In the last two minutes, Nick Tyson had changed everything.

Sara had never considered herself impulsive or prone to making bad decisions. She'd had relationships in the past, but no man had ever made her ache. If only her heart would stop pounding, she could think long enough to do the right thing and pull away.

She was vaguely aware of a crack of thunder outside. The wind rushing through the trees. She could hear Nick breathing hard. But all of it was nearly drowned out by the jackhammer rhythm of her heart. It was too much. Too powerful. Too *breathtaking*. And far too dangerous to continue...

LINDA CASTILLO

IN THE
DEAD OF NIGHT

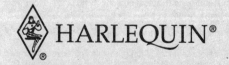

HARLEQUIN®

TORONTO • NEW YORK • LONDON
AMSTERDAM • PARIS • SYDNEY • HAMBURG
STOCKHOLM • ATHENS • TOKYO • MILAN • MADRID
PRAGUE • WARSAW • BUDAPEST • AUCKLAND

ISBN-13: 978-0-373-88794-1
ISBN-10:   0-373-88794-9

IN THE DEAD OF NIGHT

This edition published by arrangement with Harlequin Books S.A.

® and TM are trademarks of the publisher. Trademarks indicated with ® are registered in the United States Patent and Trademark Office, the Canadian Trade Marks Office and in other countries.

www.eHarlequin.com

Printed in U.S.A.

ABOUT THE AUTHOR

Linda Castillo knew at a very young age that she wanted to be a writer—and penned her first novel at the age of thirteen. She is a winner of numerous writing awards, including the Holt Medallion, the Golden Heart, the Daphne du Maurier, as well as earning a nomination for the prestigious RITA® Award.

Linda loves writing edgy romantic suspense novels that push the envelope and take her readers on a roller-coaster ride of breathtaking romance and thrilling suspense. She resides in Texas with her husband, four loveable dogs and an Appaloosa named George. For a complete list of her books, check out her Web site at www.lindacastillo.com. contact her at books@lindacastillo.com or write her at P.O. Box 577, Bushland, TX 79012.

Books by Linda Castillo

HARLEQUIN INTRIGUE

871—OPERATION: MIDNIGHT TANGO
890—OPERATION: MIDNIGHT ESCAPE
920—OPERATION: MIDNIGHT GUARDIAN
940—OPERATION: MIDNIGHT RENDEZVOUS
963—OPERATION: MIDNIGHT COWBOY
1000—A BABY BEFORE DAWN
1020—IN THE DEAD OF NIGHT

CAST OF CHARACTERS

Sara Douglas—Twenty years ago her parents were brutally killed. A crime Sara may have witnessed but can't remember. Will a killer stop her before she can uncover the truth?

Nick Tyson—The chief of police, he lost his wife just one year ago. But when Sara Douglas storms into his life and finds herself in danger, Nick is torn between playing it safe and giving in to the passion she invokes.

Richard Douglas—Twenty years ago he was an up-and-coming Hollywood producer. Did he murder his wife and her lover in a rage of jealousy, then turn the gun on himself? Or did a killer get away with murder?

Alexandra Douglas—She was the glamorous Hollywood wife. Did she have an affair with her husband's best friend? Or did someone cover up the truth?

Blaine Stocker—He was an up-and-coming Hollywood director with an eye for talent. But did he also have a dark side?

Brett Stocker—He wants to follow in his father's footsteps. But does he have the talent? Or will he find success any way he can?

Laurel Tyson—She never remarried after the death of her husband. Did her bitterness over his death drive her to murder?

Nicholas Tyson—Did the true-crime writer betray his best friend? Or was he murdered for another reason?

Skeeter—The caretaker is mute and seems harmless. Or is his benevolent appearance a facade?

Prologue

Sara Douglas wasn't afraid of the dark. She was a big girl, after all—almost eight years old. She didn't believe in monsters or the bogeyman or things that went bump in the night. But lying on her frilly bed, watching the lightning flicker outside her bedroom window, she was scared.

She clutched her little blue hippo and counted the seconds the way Mommy had told her. One. Two. A yelp escaped her when thunder crashed. She slapped her hand over her mouth and closed her eyes tightly. The thunder seemed to go on forever, like the approaching footsteps of some giant beast.

Sara wanted to slide into bed with her sister, but Sonia was spending the night at her friend Jonie's house. Sonia was nine years old and never got scared. She laughed at Sara's fear of thunderstorms and called her a ninny. That made Sara mad, but she still wished she were here.

The curtains at the French doors that opened to the balcony billowed with a sudden gust of wind. In the darkness they looked like restless ghosts. Sara jerked the covers up to her eyes. Another flash of lightning speared the sky. Thunder cracked so hard the windows rattled.

Throwing off the blanket, she slipped from her bed and darted to the French doors. It wasn't raining, but the treetops swayed like spindly fingers. Taking a deep breath, she ran along the balcony toward her parents' room, her bare feet slapping against the tile like little flippers.

One of the French doors to their room stood open a few inches. Yellow light slanted out like a sunray. Voices floated on the wind. Mommy and Daddy and Uncle Nicholas. Sara liked Uncle Nicholas. He smelled like peppermint gum and told funny stories that made her laugh.

Putting her eye to the two-inch opening,

she peered into the room. Mommy and Daddy and Uncle Nicholas were standing around the table in the sitting area, looking at some papers. But they weren't laughing. Their expressions gave Sara a funny feeling in her stomach. She wanted to go inside. She wanted her mommy to hold her while Uncle Nicholas told funny stories.

But Mommy was crying. Uncle Nicholas looked mad. He was shouting, the veins on his neck standing out like snakes beneath his skin. Daddy's face was red, his hands clenched into fists.

Sara wanted desperately to rush in and throw herself into her mother's arms. But she couldn't move. Her feet seemed to be frozen to the ground. She didn't know why, but the thought of going inside frightened her even more than the storm.

She started to cry. Lightning flickered. Out of the corner of her eye she saw the tree branches claw at the night sky. She set her hands over her ears to block the inevitable crash of thunder, but she knew it wouldn't help.

Thunder exploded. Three times in quick succession. So many times that Sara thought it would never stop. Holding her hands over her ears, crying, she shoved open the French door. Another kind of fear gripped her when she entered the bedroom. The kind that made her legs feel shaky and her stomach go tight.

Fear transformed into terror when she saw the gun. Death exploded from the muzzle. Once. Twice. Each shot was as bright as lightning. Louder than thunder. And more terrifying than any storm.

She saw a shocking bloom of red, as brilliant as the roses that grew in Mommy's garden. The world spun as if a giant tornado had picked her up. The room blurred into an eddy of terror and lightning and thunder.

"Mommy," Sara whispered.

When her mommy didn't answer, the night rushed in and swept her into its dark embrace.

Chapter One

The headlights of the rental car cut through rain and fog and darkness. Gripping the steering wheel, Sara Douglas inched along the narrow coast road at a snail's pace, not daring to look over the guardrail where the landscape dropped away to the rocky shore a hundred feet below.

The house had been calling to her for quite some time. Years, in fact, but Sara had never heeded that nagging little voice. Her job as a costume designer kept her far too busy to listen to frivolous voices inside her head. Certainly not when it came to the terrible chain of events that had shattered her life twenty years ago.

The phone call two days ago had changed everything.

Even now, the memory of the electronically altered voice sent a chill skittering up her spine. Why would someone call her and dredge up a past she'd spent a lifetime trying to forget? Who would go to such lengths to hide their identity and why? Sara intended to find out.

Midnight was not the best time to arrive at a sprawling old mansion you haven't seen for two decades. She'd planned on arriving in the light of day, but her flight from San Diego to San Francisco had been delayed due to mechanical problems. She'd taken a puddle jumper to the Shelter Cove Airport, a tiny facility that served much of northwestern California known as the Lost Coast. By the time she retrieved her luggage and rented a car, it was nearly ten o'clock.

A leaning mailbox overgrown with a tangle of vines alerted her that she'd reached her destination. She turned the car into the weed-riddled driveway. The old Douglas mansion loomed before her like some aging Hollywood actress. Shrouded in mystery and glamour and scandal, the house was perched high above the rocky cliffs overlooking the Pacific Ocean. The old place seemed to cry as it looked out over the black expanse of sea. Twenty-five years ago Sara's father, Richard Douglas—an up-and-coming Hollywood producer at the time—designed and built it for his family. A dream home that should have been filled with children and laughter and happiness.

A double murder and suicide five years later turned his dream into a nightmare, the mansion into a dark legend and the setting for even darker stories.

Sara and her sister, Sonia, had inherited the property. They'd rented out the old place a dozen times over the years. They'd discussed selling it more than once, even going so far as to put it on the real estate market. But the house hadn't sold. Later, the real estate agent told them no one wanted a house that had been the backdrop for the worst crime in the history of Cape Darkwood.

The headlights illuminated the battered mahogany garage door through slashing rain. Sara put the vehicle in Park and killed the engine. For an instant the only sound came from the pounding of rain on the roof.

"Welcome home," she whispered. But her

voice sounded strained in the silence of her car.

Not giving herself time to debate the wisdom of coming here tonight, she threw open the door and stepped into the driving rain. Darting to the rear of the car, she heaved her suitcase from the trunk and started toward the front door. Around her the cold air smelled of the ocean and wet foliage.

She rolled the suitcase up the slate walkway to the tall beveled-glass door and jammed her key into the lock. A single twist and the door groaned open. The odors of dust, mildew and years of neglect greeted her. She'd called ahead and had the utility companies turn on the electricity and phone. As her hand fumbled along the wall in the darkness, she fervently hoped they had.

A sigh of relief slid from her lips when her fingers found the switch and light flooded the foyer. For a moment, Sara could do nothing but stare at the majesty of the double spiral staircase. Constructed of marble and mahogany, twin stairs curved left and right to a railed balcony hall above that over-looked the grand foyer.

An onslaught of memories rushed over her. Her dad standing in the hall with his arms wrapped around her mother. The sound of laughter as she and Sonia rode their sleeping bags down the slick marble steps in a race to the bottom. She could practically smell the roses her mother picked every morning and arranged in a vase on the console table.

In a flash, the memories were gone, replaced by the emptiness of a house that had been vacant for so long there was no life left inside it.

Sara's boots clicked smartly against the marble tile as she crossed to the formal dining room. She flipped the light switch and for an instant she could only stand there as the grandeur of the room washed over her. A crystal chandelier iced with cobwebs cast prisms of light onto an oblong table draped with a dusty tarp. A floor-to-ceiling window looked out over a garden that had once abounded with roses and wildflowers, neat rows of herbs and the ornate Victorian gazebo Daddy and Uncle Nicholas had built that last summer. Little did they know that by fall all three of them would be dead—and her father would be accused of murder and suicide.

For twenty years Sara had believed that. She'd hated her father for stealing her childhood and shattering her happiness. For two decades she'd held that hatred close; she'd clung to it because she'd needed someone to blame. Someone to hate so she could lock all those old emotions into a compartment and get on with her life.

The phone call had brought it all rushing back, like black water backing up in a drain.

Leaving her suitcase in the dining room, she went through the first level of the house, turning on lights as she went. Some of the rooms didn't have lamps, but there was enough light for her to see that the interior had fallen in to disrepair. In her father's study, she walked along the floor-to-ceiling shelves, wondering what had happened to his collection of books. The scents of lemon oil, fragrant cigars and the leather of his chair drifted to her, but they were only memories. An arched hall took her to the bathroom. Several marble tiles on one wall had fallen to the floor and broken. Rust-colored water dripped from the ceiling, forming a puddle the size of a saucer on the floor. In the semi-darkness, the stain looked like blood.

"Don't even go there," she muttered, refusing to let her imagination take flight.

She lugged her suitcase up the stairs. Her heart pitter-pattered in her chest when she shoved open the door to her old bedroom and turned on the light. For an instant she expected to see twin beds with matching pink comforters and frilly pillows. Carved pine furniture. A purple bean-bag chair and a dollhouse as big as a Volkswagen.

Instead she was met with a queen-size bed and an antique cherry bureau that was covered with dust. A tarnished brass lamp sat upon a lone night table. Fresh linens rested on a wingback chair. It was the only room in which the furniture wasn't covered.

Sara was glad she'd called ahead and told the caretaker, a retiree by the name of Skeeter Jenks, that she would be staying the week. She and Sonia had been sending him a small check each month for maintenance. She thought about the leak in the bathroom and made a mental note to call him the next morning.

Setting her suitcase on the bed, Sara unpacked her clothes and toiletries. She'd just hung the last pair of jeans in the closet when the lights flickered and went out. She knew it was silly—she was *not* afraid of storms—but her heart went into overdrive when she was suddenly plunged into darkness.

"Lovely," she muttered.

Nothing to be alarmed about, a shaky little voice assured her. The mansion was old and practically derelict. More than likely, lightning or the wind had taken out a telephone pole. Or maybe she'd turned on too many lights and overloaded the fuse box.

Thankful she'd had the foresight to bring a flashlight, she went to the night table and pulled it from the drawer, hoping that the caretaker kept candles and fuses on hand.

She jumped at a deafening crack of thunder. Her laugh came too quickly and sounded forced. She was not afraid of storms. Really, she wasn't.

Dim light filtered in through the French

doors and within seconds her eyes adjusted to the inky blackness. The din of rain against the roof seemed louder in the darkness, the shadows more menacing. The wind whistled around the wrought-iron rails of the balcony. The silhouettes of the trees outside swayed in the gale. Somewhere in the house, she heard banging. A shutter? Or was it something else?

Using the flashlight, she made her way to the hall. The steps creaked beneath her feet as she descended the stairs and entered the foyer. The banging grew louder. She swept the beam right toward the kitchen. It was just the wind, she told herself. A piece of siding torn loose by the storm. But the flashlight beam trembled.

Thrusting the flashlight out before her like a weapon, she made her way to the kitchen. It was a cavernous room with cobalt tile countertops and intricately designed rosewood cabinetry. Once upon a time, it had been state-of-the-art. Her parents had enjoyed cooking and entertaining. Sara had spent many an afternoon sitting at the counter while her parents hovered over fancy canapés and hors d'oeuvres she couldn't pronounce.

Dim light spilled in through the arched window above the sink. During the day the window offered a stunning view of a turbulent sea. Tonight, it held darkness and shadows and a vague threat Sara didn't want to acknowledge.

Setting the flashlight on the counter, she went through each drawer. Relief slid through her when she finally unearthed a half-burned candle and a box of wooden matches.

"Who says I don't have all the luck."

She found a saucer in the cupboard, set the candle on it and lit the wick. Yellow light cast flickering images on the walls. Picking up the flashlight, she turned toward the utility room. She was midway through the kitchen when movement in her peripheral vision stopped her dead in her tracks.

Gasping, Sara spun. Her heart slammed against her ribs when she saw a shadow pass quickly past the window. She stumbled back, adrenaline burning her gut. The flashlight slipped from her hand and clattered to the floor.

Quickly, she snatched it up, but the bulb had gone out. She tapped it against the heel of her palm. When she glanced back at the window, the shadow was gone.

A terrible uneasiness stole over her. Someone was out there; she was sure of it. But why would they be at the back window of a vacant old house on a night like this? Vandals? Teenagers looking for a place to hang out? Or was something more ominous in the works?

The memory of the phone call flicked through her mind, conjuring a tinge of fear. Had she locked the front door? Was the garage locked? What about the patio doors?

Setting her hand on the cell phone clipped to her waistband, she doused the candle, knowing she would be less visible to an intruder in total darkness.

Never taking her eyes off the window, she backed from the kitchen. Her heart hammered as she moved silently through the hall toward the staircase. She could hear herself breathing hard. Blood roared like a jet engine in her ears. She passed the front door. Through the beveled glass, lightning flashed with blinding intensity, illuminating a tall figure draped in black and dripping with rain. A scream tore from her throat. She scrambled back, her hand shooting to the cell phone at her waist. The door flew open with a burst of wind and rain.

"Stop right there," came a deep male voice.

Gripping her cell phone like a lifeline, she spun and ran for her life. Tearing through the foyer, she rounded the staircase and took the steps two at a time. All the while she tried desperately to remember if there was a lock on the bedroom door.

She heard the intruder behind her as she reached the upstairs landing. Heavy footsteps. A hint of labored breathing. The knowledge that she was alone with someone who could very well mean her harm. Her fingers trembled violently as she stabbed 911 into her cell.

"Stop! Cape Darkwood PD!"

The words barely registered over the jumble of fear. She dashed into the bedroom, spun to slam the door. But the man stuck his foot in. "Take it easy," he said.

Facing the door, Sara stumbled back. In a small corner of her mind she heard the dispatcher's voice coming over her cell phone. "There's a prowler in my house!" she screamed.

The bedroom door swung open. The yellow beam of a flashlight cut through the darkness. The man stood silhouetted in the doorway. Sara looked around wildly for a weapon. Finding nothing, she glanced at the cell phone in her hand and threw it with all her might.

He ducked, but wasn't fast enough. The phone struck the left side of his face. Grunting, he lifted his hand to his cheekbone.

"The police are on the way!" she cried.

Spotting the lamp on the night table, she snatched it up and mentally prepared herself to use it if he got any closer.

"I *am* the damn police," he snapped. "Calm down."

The words penetrated the veil of shock, slowed the hard rush of fear. He illuminated his face with the flashlight beam, and Sara lowered the lamp.

"I'm a cop," he repeated. "Put down the lamp."

He didn't *look* like a cop. Wearing blue jeans and a T-shirt beneath a dark raincoat, he looked more like the villain in a slasher film. The thought made her shudder.

"I—I want to see your badge," she managed.

"Keep your hands where I can see them." He shone the light at her, sweeping it from her head to her feet. "Who are you and what are you doing here?"

"I own this place," she said.

Sliding a badge from the pocket of his trench, he shoved it at her. "You're the homeowner?"

"That's what I said."

"Show me some ID." Tilting his head slightly, he spoke into a lapel mike. "This is zero-two-four. I'm ten-twenty-three. Over."

"Whatcha got, Chief?" crackled a tinny male voice.

"Cancel that ten-fourteen, will you?"

"Roger that."

Convinced this man was indeed a cop, Sara sidled to the bed and pulled her driver's license from her wallet. "You scared the hell out of me," she snapped as she crossed to him and held it out for him to read.

He shone the beam on her license. "Sara Douglas." He said her name as if it left a bad taste in his mouth.

"Th-there was a prowler," she said. "I saw him. At the kitchen window. A man."

Dipping his head slightly, he pinched the bridge of his nose. "How long ago?"

"A minute. Maybe two."

"That was probably me."

"Oh." Sara choked out a nervous laugh, releasing some of the tension that had built up inside her.

He frowned, apparently not seeing any humor in the situation. Maybe because he had a bump the size of a quarter on his left cheekbone from where she'd thrown the cell phone.

"I'm sorry I threw the phone at you."

"Yeah." He touched the bump. "I'll let you know if I decide to arrest you for assaulting a cop."

"You're kidding, right?"

He didn't answer, and Sara found herself wishing she could see his face better.

"What are you doing here?" she asked.

"A 911 call came in about twenty minutes ago. Someone reported seeing lights up here."

Realization dawned. "Someone thought *I* was a prowler?"

"This place has been vacant for quite a few years. Neighbors aren't used to seeing any kind of activity up here. Unless, of course, it has to do with ghosts."

The word hung in the air like a bad joke. "Ghosts?"

"Word around town is that this place is haunted."

"That's pretty ridiculous." Her laugh held no humor.

"Considering what happened up here." He lifted a shoulder, let it drop. "People love a good ghost story."

Or a murder mystery, she thought.

He shoved the badge back into his pocket. She caught a glimpse of a pistol and leather shoulder holster. But even more dangerous than the weapon was the man himself. He was built like a distance runner. Tall with narrow hips and long, muscular legs encased in snug denim. The navy T-shirt was damp from the rain and clung to an abdomen that regularly saw the inside of a gym.

"So are you planning on hitting me with that?"

Realizing she was still clutching the lamp, Sara returned it to the bedside table. "I thought you were an intruder."

"Good thing for you I'm not." He motioned toward the lamp. "Wouldn't do much good against a gun."

Sara didn't know what to say to that; she knew firsthand the damage a gun could do.

"I didn't mean to spook you," he said. "You okay?"

"Just a little rattled. Electricity went out."

"Lightning took out a transformer down on Wind River Road. Crews are out, but it's pretty remote out here. Could take a while."

"Lovely."

"Do you have a flashlight or candles?"

"I dropped the flashlight and broke it, but I think there are candles in the kitchen."

"I'll stay long enough for you to get a few lit if you'd like."

"Not that I'm afraid of ghosts or anything."

"Of course not." Touching the brim of his cap, he left the bedroom and started for the stairs.

Feeling silly for having overreacted, Sara followed.

"Where are you from?" he asked as they descended the stairs.

"San Diego."

At the kitchen, he moved aside and motioned her ahead, shining the flashlight so she could see. Sara went to the candle she'd left on the counter, relit it, then began rummaging for more.

"Alexandra and Richard Douglas were your parents?"

That he knew her parents' first names shouldn't have surprised her, but it did. Cape Darkwood was a small town, after all. She looked up from the drawer. In the candle-light, she was able to get a better look at his face. An odd sense of familiarity niggled at the back of her mind. Her hands paused as she reached for a second candle. She wasn't sure why, but her stomach went taut in anticipation of some unexpected and ugly surprise. "Yes, they were my parents. Why?"

"I used to know them. My parents knew them, actually. A long time ago."

Sensing there was more coming, she stopped rummaging and looked at him over her shoulder. His eyes met hers. A little too curious. A little too intense. A keen awareness of him rippled through her. She wanted to blame it on the darkness. The storm. The strangeness of the house. Whatever the case, he was one of the most disconcerting men she'd ever met.

"I used to know you, too," he added.

Sara faced him, certain she would have remembered meeting this man. He had one of the most memorable faces she'd ever encountered. Definitely unforgettable eyes. "I don't think so."

"It's been a while," he said.

"I didn't get your name." The words came out as a whisper.

"I'm Chief of Police Nick Tyson." He stuck out his hand. "Your father shot and killed my father the same night he murdered your mother."

Chapter Two

Sara stared at Nick, her mind reeling. She'd known that at some point she would have to face this. The past. The people whose lives her father had ripped apart all those years ago. But to face this man now—a man whose life had been shattered by the actions of her father—seemed a cruel twist of fate.

"Nicky?" she said.

"People don't usually call me that now." His grin transformed hardened features into a hint of the boy she'd once known. A rough-and-tumble kid with black hair and eyes the color of the Pacific. Her memory stirred like a beast that had been hibernating for two decades. She'd been seven years old. Twelve-year-old Nicky Tyson had talked her into playing hide and seek, but when she'd closed her eyes, instead of running and hiding, he'd stolen a kiss. Her first kiss from a boy. It had been innocent, but made a huge impact on Sara.

Funny that she would remember something so silly at a moment like this. But then she'd blocked a lot of things that happened that last summer.

The man standing before her was nothing like the ornery kid who'd pestered—and secretly charmed—her. There was nothing remotely innocent about him. His eyes were still the color of the sea, but now it was a stormy sea, all crashing surf and churning waves and water the color of slate. Beneath the brim of the Cape Darkwood PD cap, his black hair was military-short. He might have looked clean-cut if not for the day's growth of beard and the hard gleam in his eyes.

"Surprised?" he asked.

Realizing his hand was still extended and she had yet to take it, Sara reached out. "I don't know what to say."

His hand encompassed hers completely. His grip was firm. She got the impression of

calluses and strength tempered with a gen-
tleness that belied the obvious strength.

"Hello would suffice," he said.

An awkward silence descended. Intellectually, Sara knew what her father had done
wasn't her fault; she'd been a little girl at the
time. But it was disconcerting to think that
this man's father had been her mother's illicit
lover. That her father had murdered Nicholas
Tyson in a jealous rage then turned the gun
on himself. That was the story the newspapers had reported, anyway.

Sara was no longer sure she believed it.

She studied Nick Tyson and thought about
the call she'd received two days ago. The
electronically disguised voice that told her
Richard Douglas hadn't murdered anyone on
that terrible June night. Had there been a
fourth person involved as the caller inti-
mated? A person filled with hatred and a
secret that was now up to her to expose—or
disprove?

The memory of the voice spread gooseflesh over her arms. She studied Nick's face.
Familiar now, but somehow every bit as
threatening. His was the face of a cop. Hard,

knowing eyes filled with suspicion, cool distance and an intensity that thoroughly unnerved. She couldn't help but wonder if, as a policeman himself, he'd ever doubted the scenario the police had pieced together.

"Ah, you're in luck."

The words jerked her from her reverie. She let go of his hand. He must have seen the uncertainty on her face because he motioned toward the drawer she'd opened. "Another candle," he said.

"Oh. Right."

His eyes shone black in the semidarkness. She could feel them on her, probing, wondering. Wondering what? Why she was back? Or was he wondering if a capacity for violence was inherited?

"I should probably check the fuse box while I'm here," he said.

"We wouldn't want those ghosts getting any ideas."

He gave her a half smile. "Everyone knows they do their best work in the dark."

The tension drained from her body when he started toward the utility room and, beyond, the garage where the fuse box was located.

Using the dim light slanting in through the window, she began searching for another plate or saucer to use as a candleholder.

"Fuses look fine."

She jolted at the closeness of his voice and nearly dropped the saucer she'd found. He was standing right behind her, so close she could smell the piney-woods scent of his aftershave. For the first time she realized just how tall he was. At least six-three or maybe six-four. He towered over her five-foot-three-inch frame. Uncle Nicholas had been tall....

Nick stared at her intently. "You're not still afraid of storms, are you?"

"Of course not," she said a little too quickly.

One side of his mouth curved. "Looks like you'll have to ride this one out in the dark."

"Thanks for coming by. And for checking the fuses." She wanted to say more, but what? *Thank you for not hating me. I'm sorry my father ruined your childhood. Oh, and by the way, he didn't do it....*

The words flitted through her mind, but she didn't voice them. Even though she was no longer convinced her father had done anything wrong that night, she needed to figure out who to trust—and find proof of her suspicions—before going to the police.

"Just doing my job." His gaze flicked to the saucer in her hand. Usurping it from her, he set the candle on it and dug out a match. "This should help keep the ghosts away."

"If you believe in that sort of thing."

"Don't you?"

"Not for a second. Don't tell me you do."

"I guess it depends on the ghost." He set the saucer on the counter. "Hopefully the utility crews will get the transformer up and working in the next couple of hours."

"Does the electricity go out often up here?"

"They don't call this stretch of beach the Lost Coast for nothing." He stood there a moment, studying her. "How long will you be in town?"

"I'm not sure," she answered. "A few days. Maybe a week."

"Any particular reason you're back?"

Sara wished it were lighter so she could gauge his expression. Was it an idle question? Or was he uneasy that someone was sniffing around a mystery that, in the minds of a few, had never been solved? Somewhere in the back of her mind, the caller's voice echoed eerily. *Don't trust anyone....*

"Family business," she said vaguely.

"I see." But his expression told her he didn't. "How's your sister?"

"Sonia's doing great. She and her husband live in Los Angeles now. She thinks I'm a nut for staying here."

"It's not exactly the Ritz."

She smiled, but it felt brittle on her face. "I think she was more concerned about how the citizens of Cape Darkwood would react."

As if realizing to whom she was referring, Nick sobered and shoved his hands into his pockets. "There might be a few people in this town who can't differentiate between what your father did twenty years ago and you."

"What are you saying?"

"Some people have short memories and small minds. If you run into any hostility, give me a call."

"I hope I don't." But Sara knew she probably

would. Emotions had run high and hot in Cape Darkwood after her father had allegedly shot and killed his pretty young wife and her lover, then himself, leaving two little girls without parents, a little boy without a father.

She looked at Nick. "It seems like if anyone in this town has a right to be angry with the Douglas family, it's you."

"I wasn't the only one hurt that night."

The statement made Sara think of Nick's mother. Laurel Tyson had been widowed at the age of thirty and left with a mountain of bills and a young boy to raise. Sara had been too distraught to remember much about her parents' funeral, but she would never forget the look of hatred in Laurel Tyson's eyes.

"How's your mother, Nick?"

"She's doing fine. Owns an antique shop and a couple of bed-and-breakfasts in town." His expression darkened. "But then, you knew about the B&Bs, didn't you?"

Sara nodded.

"Then you've already realized it might be a good idea for you to steer clear of her."

His meaning was not lost on Sara. She'd often wondered if Laurel Tyson had recovered from the grief and scandal surrounding her husband's murder.

"Thanks for the warning."

He studied her a moment longer, then touched the brim of his cap. "Welcome back, Sara."

At that he started for the door, leaving in his wake the smell of pine and rain and the undeniable feeling that she would see him again.

THE MEMORY of her sultry perfume still danced in his head when Nick climbed into his cruiser. Sara Douglas was a far cry from the freckle-faced little girl he'd played hide and seek with some twenty years ago. She'd grown into a gypsy-eyed beauty with a throaty laugh and a body any Hollywood actress would give her right hand to possess.

As a man, he'd enjoyed seeing her, talking to her. *Touching her,* an annoying little voice chimed in. But as a cop, he knew her return to Cape Darkwood spelled trouble. He couldn't help but wonder why she'd really come back. He didn't buy the family-business bit. Why would she fly all the way from San Diego to Cape Darkwood and spend a week in a dilapidated mansion when most business matters could be handled via phone? The mansion was barely habitable. Especially taking into consideration what had happened there twenty years ago.

But Nick knew why she hadn't stayed at one of the bed-and-breakfasts in town. His mother owned both of them. Sara must have done her homework and realized it would have been an uncomfortable situation to say the least.

Thoughts of his mother elicited a sigh. He'd lied to her when he'd said his mother was doing okay. Laurel Tyson had never recovered from the events of that summer night twenty years ago. Nick had never been sure if her bitterness stemmed from the fact that her husband had been having an affair or that he'd been gunned down for it. Whatever the case, her happiness had ended that night right along with Nick's childhood. Neither of them needed the past dredged up.

As he started the engine and pulled out of the driveway, he decided Sara Douglas bore watching. He was the chief of police, after all. It was his job to keep an eye on people.

He didn't want to admit that his interest went a tad beyond professional concern. Twenty years ago he'd had a crush on her the size of California. In a kid-sister kind of way. He knew it was crazy, but the old attraction was still there, as clear and sharp as the dawn sky after a storm. Only now, there wasn't anything kid-sister about it. Nick wasn't happy about it. He had a sixth sense when it came to trouble. Sara Douglas had trouble written all over that shapely body of hers in big, bold letters.

As he pulled onto Wind River Road and started for town, he decided it would be best for everyone involved if she let the ghosts of the past rest in peace. The citizens of Cape Darkwood—including him—would rest a hell of a lot easier when she went back to San Diego where she belonged.

Chapter Three

She saw blood, stark and red against pale flesh. The metallic smell surrounded her, sickened her. Horror punched through layers of shock. She couldn't breathe, couldn't scream.

"Mommy," she whimpered. "Wake up. I'm scared. Wake up!"

Sara shook her, but her mother didn't stir. Feeling something warm and sticky between her fingers, Sara looked down at her hands.

Blood.

Her child's mind rebelled against what she saw. Against what she knew in her heart. Against the terror of knowing her mommy wasn't ever going to open her eyes again.

Ten feet away her daddy lay on the floor, his head surrounded by a slick of red. Next to him, Uncle Nicholas lay sprawled on his back. His eyes were open, but when she called out to him he didn't answer. Why wouldn't he answer her? Why wouldn't he wake up and tell her everything was going to be okay? That they were just playing? Making a movie?

Thunder cracked like a thousand gunshots. Sara screamed and crawled to her mother's side, curled against her. "Mommy," she choked out the name and began to cry. "Please wake up. I'm so scared."

Outside the French doors lightning flashed, turning night to day. Beyond, a man in a long, black coat stood in the driving rain, staring at her. He held something dark in his hand. A gun, she realized. It had a shiny white grip, like the ones cowboys used in movies. But he was no Lone Ranger; he was a bad man.

Her heart beat out of control when he raised the gun and pointed it at her. For an interminable moment, the storm went silent. All she could hear was the freight-train hammer of her pulse. Somewhere deep inside she knew he was going to hurt her, the same way he'd hurt her mommy and daddy. She didn't want to go to sleep and never wake up. Closing her eyes, Sara buried her face in her mother's shirt.

Another crack of thunder rattled the windows.

When she opened her eyes and raised her head, the bad man was gone.

And she began to scream.

Sara sat bolt upright, her heart pounding, her body slicked with sweat. The old fear thrashed inside her like the reemergence of a long-dormant illness.

Blowing out a shaky breath, she lay back in the pillows and willed her heart to slow. It had been a long time since she'd had the nightmare. After the deaths of her parents, it had taken more than six years of therapy before she could sleep through the night. But as she'd entered her teens, Sara had finally begun to heal. Slowly but surely, her mind had shoved the horrors of that night into a small, dark corner where they had remained.

Until now.

This particular dream had been incredibly vivid, conjuring all of her senses and a barrage of emotions. In the past, the nightmare had evolved around her finding the bodies of her parents and Nicholas Tyson. She'd never dreamed of the man with the gun.

Twenty years ago, a detective by the name of Henry James had investigated the case. He gave her a cherry lollipop every time he questioned her. As days spun into weeks and Sara began to understand what happened, she'd realized Detective James believed she'd witnessed the murders.

It had been a heavy burden for an eight-year-old. Sara spent years trying to remember. She'd even undergone hypnosis. But the memory—if there was one—refused to emerge. She never understood how she could forget something so vitally important, especially if the real murderer got away scot-free.

Eventually, the police pieced together the events of that night, ruled the crimes a murder-suicide and the case was closed. Now, Sara was left to wonder if they'd been wrong.

Was the man in the long black coat a figment of her imagination? Perhaps it was her mind's way of redeeming her father? Or was he part of a blocked memory resurfacing?

Troubled by the notion of a killer getting away with the murders of three good people, Sara slipped into her robe, crossed to the French doors and flung them open. Beyond, the Pacific churned in a kaleidoscope of blue and green capped with white. The beach sang to her with the crashing notes of a well-remembered and much-loved ballad. She breathed in deeply, clearing her head and savoring the scent of last night's rain.

She craved coffee as she descended the staircase and was glad she'd had the foresight to tuck a few single servings into her bag. After brewing coffee, she carried a steaming mug to the redwood deck.

The Adirondack furniture that had belonged to her parents had long since been sold. But the view was the same and so stunning that for a moment she could do nothing but stare. Whitecaps rode a violent sea of midnight blue. Leaning against the rail, she looked out over the rocky cliff at the battered rocks below. Mesmerized, she watched the fog bank retreat into the sea like the spirits of long-lost sailors.

She wasn't sure why the scene reminded her of Nick Tyson. Something about his eyes and the ocean. Sara wasn't given to noticing inconsequential details about men. But even in last night's darkness, she'd discerned the reckless male beauty lurking beneath a mild facade that would be dangerous to an unwary woman. Sara was glad she didn't fall into that category.

The ringing of the phone in the kitchen drew her from her reverie. Surprised, taking her mug with her, she went through the French doors. Expecting her sister, she picked up on the third ring. "Checking up on me?"

"You came."

Shock rippled through her at the familiar, electronically-altered voice. "How did you get this number?"

"I have resources, but that doesn't matter."

"Who are you?" She posed the question, but knew he wouldn't answer.

"All that matters is finding the truth."

"What truth?"

"About what really happened that night."

"The police investigated and closed the case."

"The police don't know everything."

Her heart beat too fast in her chest, and she took a deep breath to calm herself. "Stop beating around the bush and tell me what you know."

He was silent for so long she feared he'd hung up. "Find the manuscript, Sara. It will explain everything."

"What manuscript?" It was the first time she'd heard of a manuscript. "What are you talking about?"

"Find it."

"Who are you?" she whispered. "Why are you calling me? Why now?"

"You're the only one left." Another silence. "You saw him, after all."

Her heart pounded harder, like a frightened animal trapped in her chest. "I—I didn't see anyone." But she couldn't stop thinking about the nightmare—and the man with the gun.

"Be careful," the voice whispered. *"Trust no one."*

"Please, tell me who you are. Tell me why you're calling, dredging all of this up now."

The line went dead.

Uneasiness climbed over her, like a scatter of ants over her body. Frustrated and uneasy, Sara cradled the phone. "Crackpot," she whispered.

But she knew that probably wasn't the case. She wouldn't have taken a week off and flown from San Diego to Cape Darkwood on the word of some prankster. Somewhere deep inside, she *knew* the police had made a mistake. But how did the caller play into all of this? Was there some type of manuscript that would prove her father had been falsely accused? How was she supposed to find it?

She'd come back to this house, this town, to uncover the truth. She owed it to herself. To her sister. To her parents. It wasn't going to be easy, but she knew where she had to start. She knew the key to unlocking the truth might very well lie in the nightmares of the past.

THE CORNER NOOK was exactly the kind of shop Sara would have frequented had she been on an antique-buying excursion. She'd inherited her love of old things from her mother. Even as a child, she'd enjoyed browsing the stores and wondering about the history of the trinkets they brought home.

Sandwiched between a coffee shop and the Red Door Bed-and-Breakfast, the Corner Nook was as inviting as a tropical beach on a hot day. But Sara felt no anticipation as she parked the rental car curbside. Dread curdled in her gut as she started down the cobblestone walk.

The bell on the door jingled merrily when she entered, the aromas of vanilla and citrus pleasing her nose. Having recently furnished her first home, Sara had spent hours perusing antique shops. But she'd never seen such an eclectic collection in one place. To her right an entire wall was dedicated to Hollywood nostalgia. A nice collection of celebrity cookbooks jammed the top shelf. Beyond, a dress once worn by Marilyn Monroe flowed elegantly over an ancient wooden mannequin. Sara was so caught up in admiring the wares, she didn't hear the proprietor approach.

"Are you looking for something special?"

She spun at the sound of the rich voice and found herself facing a tall, elegantly dressed woman. She caught a glimpse of silver hair and midnight-blue eyes before recognition slammed home.

Laurel Tyson pressed a slender, ring-clad hand to her chest and stepped back, her face going white. "Alex."

The name came out as little more than a puff of breath, but Sara heard it. Her mother's name was Alexandra, but everyone had called her Alex. "Mrs. Tyson, it's Sara Douglas."

The woman blinked as if waking from a nightmare. Something dark and unnerving flashed in her eyes. "What earthly reason could you possibly have for coming into my shop?"

"If you have a moment, I'd like to ask you a few questions."

"I have nothing to say to you."

Sara hesitated, surprised by the degree of the woman's hostility. But she hadn't traveled six hundred miles to give up at the first sign of resistance. "I want to talk to you about what happened…."

Laurel's eyes went flat. "I have nothing to say to you about that night."

"I know this is difficult. It's been hard for me, too. But if you'd just hear me out."

"*Difficult* is not the right word, Sara. Your family has hurt mine enough. Now if you'll excuse me, I have customers."

There weren't any other customers in the shop. Sara didn't want to upset her, but she desperately needed information. Laurel had been her mother's best friend. She might know something that could help her sort through the mystery. If only she could get her to listen.

"I may have new information about what really happened," Sara said.

"What *really* happened?" The woman choked out a sound that was part laugh, part grunt. "I already know what happened."

"I think the police may have made a mistake."

"How dare you." Laurel's lips peeled back in an ugly parody of a smile. "You have some nerve walking into my place of business and making wild insinuations."

"All I want is to find the truth," Sara said honestly.

"The truth, darling, is that your father was a killer and your mother was a whore."

Sara recoiled at the viciousness of the

words. A knot curled in her chest. Under any other circumstances, she would have backed off, found another source of information. But Laurel Tyson was Sara's strongest link to her parents and what might have taken place that night. "I know you were hurt, but if you'd just give me a minute—"

"I've given you enough." Laurel turned away. "Get out."

Sara reached out to touch the other woman's arm. Laurel spun with the speed of a striking cobra. She shoved Sara's hand away with so much force that Sara's fingers brushed a porcelain figurine and sent it crashing to the floor. The delicate china shattered into a hundred pieces.

"See what you've done?"

"Mrs. Tyson, I didn't mean to upset you." Sara looked down at the broken statuette, truly sorry, and wondered how the situation had spiraled out of control so quickly. "Please, let me pay for—"

"You'll never be able to pay enough." Angrily, Laurel gestured toward the door, her hand shaking. "Now, get out or I'll call the police."

Vaguely, Sara heard the bell on the door jingle as another customer entered the shop. In a last-ditch effort to get the woman to listen, she lowered her voice to a whisper. "I have reason to believe my father didn't kill anyone that night."

The woman's hand shot out so quickly Sara didn't have time to brace. Laurel's palm struck Sara's cheek hard enough to snap her head back. The sound was like the crack of a bullwhip in the silence of the shop.

Sara reeled backward. She would have fallen if strong arms hadn't caught her from behind. "Easy," came a familiar male voice. "I've got you."

Nick Tyson steadied her, then quickly thrust himself between the two women. "What the hell is going on here?" he demanded, his angry gaze flicking from Sara to his mother.

Laurel thrust a finger at Sara. "She's not welcome here. I want her to leave. Now."

Nick's gaze went to Sara. He tilted his head as if to get a better look at her. His eyes narrowed to slits, and she got the sinking sensation that he was going to take his mother's side. He surprised her by asking, "Do you want to press charges?"

"You wouldn't dare," Laurel breathed.

"Try me," Nick shot back, but he never took his eyes from Sara.

"No." Shaken and embarrassed, Sara started for the door.

The older woman's gaze swept over her as she brushed past. An emotion Sara could only describe as hatred gleamed in her eyes. "You're just like her," Laurel said icily. "You look like her. You sound like her. You lie just like her."

"That's enough," Nick snapped.

Sara told herself the words didn't hurt. But deep inside, they cut as proficiently as any knife.

By the time she reached the door she was dangerously close to tears. There was no way in hell she'd let Laurel Tyson see her cry.

She yanked open the door. Nick called out her name, but Sara didn't stop. She barely noticed the slashing rain as she ran to her car. Opening the driver's-side door, she slid behind the wheel and jammed the key into the ignition. All the while, Laurel's words rang in her ears.

…your father was a killer and your mother was a whore.

Those were the words that hurt the most, she realized. She'd loved her parents desperately. To have their names tarnished when they weren't there to defend themselves outraged and offended her deeply.

"You're wrong about them." Sara jammed the car into Reverse.

When she glanced in the rearview mirror, her heart stopped dead in her chest. "Oh my God."

Hitting the brake, she turned. Blood-red letters streaked from the rain were scrawled messily on the rear window.

Curiosity killed the cat.

Chapter Four

Nick's temper was still pumping when he ran from the shop to catch Sara. He spotted her rental car just as she was backing away from the curb. He sprinted toward it. "Sara! Wait!"

Of course, she couldn't hear him with the windows rolled up tightly against the deluge of rain. But to his surprise, the car jerked to a halt. He waited, expecting her to pull back into the parking place, but the car remained still, idling halfway into the street.

Only when a car horn sounded from the street did he realize she was blocking traffic. Crossing to the driver's-side door, Nick bent and tapped on the glass. He wasn't sure why he'd run into the rain after her. He wasn't even sure what he was going to say. All he knew was that he didn't want to leave things the way they were.

The window hummed down. He started to tell her to pull forward when he noticed her shell-shocked expression. If he hadn't been a cop, he might not have discerned the pale cast of her complexion, her white-knuckled grip on the steering wheel or the way her eyes kept flicking to the rear window.

"I don't have anything to say to you," she said.

"Yeah, well, I've got something to say to you." He motioned toward the parking meter. "Pull in."

Shaking her head, she put the car in gear and eased it back into the parking space. Only when the rear window came into view did Nick notice the crude red lettering smeared on the glass. The rain had obliterated much of the letters, but there was enough left for him to make out what they spelled.

Curiosity killed the cat.

What the hell?
He stared at the words for a moment, then

strode to the window. "How long has that been there?"

"I don't know." She blew out a pent-up breath. "It wasn't there when I walked into your mother's shop."

He looked up and down the street, but the sidewalks were mostly deserted because of the rain. "Did you see anyone near your car when you walked out?"

"I was a little preoccupied but, no, I didn't notice anyone."

Realizing he was soaked, he motioned across the street. "Look, the police station is right there. I'd like for you to walk over with me so we can talk about this."

"You mean the fact that your mother slapped me? Or the adolescent cliché some clown wrote on my car?"

"Both." Nick opened her door. "Come on. I've got hot coffee."

To his surprise she acquiesced. Without speaking, they crossed the street, jumping over the torrent of water at the curb.

The police station was a small office on the first level of a redbrick building that also housed the local phone company and two apartments on the second level. Nick shoved open the wooden door, bypassed the stairs, and took Sara through a glass door and directly to the police department.

His dispatcher, administrative assistant and part-time officer glanced up from his desk when they entered.

"Damn, Chief, forget your rain suit?"

"Left it in my other bag," Nick said sardonically.

Behind him, Sara brushed rain from her jacket, but she was hopelessly soaked.

Noticing his dispatcher's curious stare, he frowned. "B.J., this is Sara Douglas." Nick glanced at Sara. "This is B. J. Lundgren, one of my officers."

"Nice to meet you." Rising, B.J. offered his hand. "You're staying up at the old Douglas mansion?"

Sara nodded and shook his hand. "Word travels fast."

"Small town." He smiled. "You're…a relative?"

"They were my parents."

"Oh." B.J. nodded. "I'm the one who took

the prowler call last night. Sorry 'bout that. Hope it didn't scare you too much."

"It's okay." Sara glanced at Nick. "The power was out and Chief Tyson let me borrow his lantern."

Nick almost smiled. B.J. hung on to every word like a pup waiting for a treat. At twenty-four, he was Nick's youngest officer and obviously enamored by Sara.

"Let me grab a towel for you." Rising, B.J. disappeared into a back room and returned with two fluffy towels. He tossed one to Nick, and handed the other to Sara.

"Thank you."

Taking the towel, Nick wiped the rain from his face and crossed to the coffee station, pouring two cups.

"That's fresh-brewed, Chief. Made it just a few minutes ago."

Nick handed one of the cups to Sara and lowered his voice. "Be careful, his coffee is lethal."

For the first time, she smiled. Nick would have smiled back, but noticed the small abrasion on her cheekbone and grimaced instead. He couldn't believe his mother had struck her. But he knew she'd never recovered from what had happened that night twenty years ago. He supposed they all bore scars. But to hold a misplaced grudge against Sara for something her father did was unconscionable. He was going to have to talk to his mother about it.

"We can talk in my office." He motioned toward the wood-paneled door at the rear of the room.

Sara headed toward Nick's office. Nick glanced back at B.J. who was doing his best not to ogle her. His deputy raised his brows up and down like Groucho Marx and gave him a thumbs-up.

"Cut it out," Nick murmured.

Walking inside, he closed the door behind them and settled behind his desk, all too aware of the faint scent of perfume on her wet skin.

Sara took the visitor's chair across from him and sipped her coffee. She'd toweled her hair, leaving it tousled and curling around her face, like wet brown silk against fine porcelain. Her brows were thin and dark and arched above big, gypsy eyes. But it was her mouth that arrested his attention and held it. Full lips the color of mulberries arched like a pretty bow. Twenty years ago he'd kissed that mouth. Even as a twelve-year-old kid, it had made one hell of an impression on him. As a man, he knew one kiss would never be enough....

"I didn't realize your mother would still harbor such intense ill feelings toward me over...what happened."

Realizing he was staring, Nick picked up his cup of coffee. "I wanted to apologize for what she did." Taking in the mark on her cheek, he grimaced. "That was inexcusable."

"Thank you." She lifted a hand as if to touch the small bruise, but let her hand drop to her lap instead.

"If you want to press charges..."

"I think everyone involved has already been hurt enough."

"Just don't think that because she's my mother I won't do my job."

"Thank you for saying that."

Leaning over, Nick dumped his remaining coffee into the ficus tree's pot. When he set the cup back on his desk, he noticed Sara watching him. "Tree doesn't seem to mind."

"I wasn't going to ask."

He smiled. "Just don't tell B.J."

She didn't smile back, but amusement glinted in her eyes.

For an instant, the only sound came from the rain hitting the glass. Nick took that moment to ask the question that had been gnawing at him since the moment he'd seen the rental car parked outside his mother's shop. "Was your visit to my mother part of the family business you're taking care of while you're here?"

"One of the reasons." She sipped coffee.

Nick's cop's instinct had been telling him all along there was more to her appearance in Cape Darkwood than she was letting on. "So what's the other reason?"

"I want you to reopen the case."

An odd mix of disbelief and disappointment gripped Nick's gut. She'd seemed so rational last night. As a cop, he appreciated rational people. Why did she have to go and spoil his opinion of her?

"What case?" he asked, knowing full well which case she was referring to, hoping he was wrong.

"The Douglas murder-suicide." She said the words as if he were dense.

"You mean the one that has been closed for twenty years?" he asked dryly.

She pursed her lips as if he were trying her patience. The feeling was mutual. If she hadn't been so damn good to look at in her snug jeans and lavender T-shirt, he might have already tossed her out of his office. But he'd always been drawn to her. A lifetime ago, the feeling had been innocent and vague. As a man there was nothing vague or innocent about what he felt for Sara Douglas. Attraction. Maybe with a hint of adult male lust mixed in.

Setting her cup on the corner of his desk, she leaned forward. "Nick, I think the police may have been wrong."

"And you think that because…?"

She hesitated, and for the first time Nick got the impression she wasn't telling him everything. That she was keeping secrets. What secrets? What could possibly have been important enough to prompt her to fly all the way from San Diego to Cape Darkwood after all the terrible things that had happened here?

"I have my reasons," she said vaguely.

"I guess it's safe to assume you're not going to make this easy and tell me what the hell you're talking about."

"Let's just say I have reason to believe there was a fourth person involved."

"A fourth person?" Intrigued, he leaned forward. "Like who?"

"I don't know."

"Then how can you be so sure there was one?"

"I'm not." Frustration tightened her mouth.

"That doesn't leave me with sufficient grounds to reopen the case."

"Maybe you could do it…unofficially."

"What does that mean?"

"You're the cop. All I'm asking is for you to take a look at the file. See if all the loose ends were tied up."

"Sara, the case was closed. I'm not real big on conspiracy theories."

"Neither am I," she said firmly. "But if certain things didn't come to light twenty years ago, don't you want to know about it?"

"Certain things like what?"

He stared at her, vaguely aware of the din of rain, that his heart rate was up just a tad. "Are you trying to tell me you've remembered something about that night?"

"No," she replied quickly.

The accepted supposition amongst the residents of Cape Darkwood was that seven-year-old Sara Douglas had witnessed the murders, but the experience had been so horrific, her young mind had blocked it. Had the memory finally resurfaced? Why wouldn't she tell him?

"If you want me to follow up, you're going to have to give me something a little bit more concrete to go on."

"I don't have anything concrete."

"Then at least level with me. Tell my why you're here. Why you came back."

"There's no hidden agenda, Nick. All I can tell you is that I came to find the truth."

"Are you telling me your father didn't kill them?"

"I'm telling you I'd like the police department to revisit the case and prove beyond a shadow of doubt that he did."

Nick thought of the words written in red on

the rear window of her car and an uncharacter-istic rise of concern went through him. "Have you told anyone else about your suspicions?"

"No." She hesitated just long enough for him to believe otherwise.

"Any idea who vandalized your car?"

"No. Kids." She shrugged. "Someone who doesn't want me poking around and asking questions."

Her answer gave him a bad feeling in the pit of his stomach.

She got to her feet. "Look, I've wasted enough of your time."

Nick rose. He knew it was silly, but he didn't want her to leave. There was a part of him that wanted to help her. But was his need to do so because of her pretty brown eyes and the way she wore those blue jeans? Or because he thought there was merit to her suspicions?

Standing behind his desk, he watched her cross to the door. "Where are you going?" he asked.

She looked at him over her shoulder. "To get something concrete and bring it back to you."

He wanted to say more, but for the life of

him the words wouldn't come. Only when she'd reached the door and gone through it did he realize what he wanted to say.

"Watch your back," he whispered.

SARA'S LEGS were still shaking when she yanked open the car door and slid behind the wheel. The words smeared on the rear window had been washed away by the rain, the same way her hope for help had been washed away by Nick's words.

...give me something a little bit more concrete to go on.

His voice rang in her ears as she backed onto the street and put the car in gear. She wasn't sure why she'd expected him to help her without question. He was a cop, after all. Cops tended to be cynical. Of course he would want something solid in order to reopen the case. Or did he have another reason for not wanting to help her?

Trust no one....

The anonymous caller's words crept over her like a chill, and she reminded herself that someone in this quaint little town could very well be a killer. If he or she knew Sara was sniffing around and asking questions, they might want to get her out of the way.

"It's going to take a lot more than some juvenile threat," she muttered.

There was one more place to go for answers. A place where secrets and emotions played no role. The Cape Darkwood Library was located just off the traffic circle in a turn-of-the-century Greek revival house that had been donated to the town by Sir Leonard Darkwood upon his death in 1926. It was a place Sara had spent many a Sunday afternoon, reading with her mom and browsing the hundreds of books.

The rain had stopped by the time she parked on the street beneath a massive elm tree and made her way up the sidewalk to the wide beveled-glass doors. Inside, the library smelled exactly as she remembered. Old paper. Lemon oil. Heated air from antique steam registers that hissed and pinged. All laced with a pleasant hint of book dust.

Though her mission wasn't the least bit enjoyable, the memories made Sara smile as she crossed to the information desk. A tiny woman wearing a maroon print dress looked at her over the tops of cat's-eye glasses. "May I help you?"

"I'm looking for archived newspaper stories."

The woman removed her glasses, her eyes narrowing. "Do you have a date in mind?"

Sara hesitated, not wanting to get too specific or else risk starting the tongues wagging in town. "I'm not sure exactly."

"Everything before June 1, 1989 is on microfiche. Everything after that date is on disk." She looked pleased with herself. "I've been working on computerizing our archives."

"This would be on microfiche," Sara said, keeping her answer purposefully vague.

"Microfiche is in the basement." She rounded the desk. "I'll show you."

Sara followed her across the marble floor, past the children's books section to a wide stairway that led to a low-ceilinged room with red carpet. A smattering of desks, a row of narrow file cabinets and a microfiche machine filled the room.

"We only have one machine left," the librarian said. "Other one went kaput last year and we didn't have budget dollars for another."

"This one will be fine. Thank you."

The woman smiled the way a not-so-kind grandmother would smile at a child from the wrong side of the tracks. "Dear, you look familiar. Are you from around here?"

Sara had never been a good liar. But for the time being she didn't want anyone to know she was back. She scrambled for an answer. "I'm from L.A., actually, and researching an article for my boss."

"Any particular subject matter?"

Murder. "History," she answered.

"I must be mistaken, then." But from the glint in her eyes, Sara wasn't sure the woman believed her. "I'll leave you to your work."

The instant the librarian was out of sight, Sara crossed to the row of file cabinets. Anticipation of getting her hands on information that wasn't rumor or hearsay bolstered her, and she scanned the labels. Each was marked with a date range. Midway down the row, she paused and pulled out the drawer she needed. Setting it on the desk, she paged through each film until she came to the dates she wanted.

The day after the murders, the *Cape*

Darkwood Press ran the first of many stories. Even now the headline made Sara shiver.

Prominent Hollywood Producer, Wife, Local Author Found Murdered.

Pulling out a small spiral notebook, Sara scanned the article, making notes as she went. The name of the lead detective who investigated the case. Possible witnesses. The journalist who reported it all.

The following day the headlines read:

Douglas Killings May Have Been Murder Suicide.

Sara read the piece with care, noting the evidence listed by police. Richard Douglas's fingerprints were on the gun, a .38 caliber revolver. The gun had fallen to the floor as if Douglas had shot himself, then dropped it.

Richard Douglas May Have Killed in a Jealous Rage....

She struggled not to let the words get to her. Though she'd only been seven years old

at the time, Sara had spent enough time with
her father to know he was a gentle man with
a kind heart. A man who kissed her nose at
bedtime and made her laugh. There was no
way that same man had killed two people
he'd cared for in cold blood.

Working quickly now, she jotted down the
name of a neighbor who'd witnessed an
argument just a week before while out
walking her dog. Emma Beasley. The newspaper reporter had evidently interviewed and
quoted her.

It was around 6:00 a.m. when I heard
Mr. Douglas shouting at his wife.
Nicholas Tyson's car was there. The
lights were on in the upstairs bedroom.
Strange goings-on in that house. Pity
with those two little girls. I guess you
never know about people.

Disgusted by the woman's unfounded as-
sumptions—and the journalist's willingness
to print them—Sara shook her head, hating
it that gossip and hearsay may have had as

much to do with the outcome of the case as the evidence itself.

Hitting the print button, she went on to the next story.

Love Triangle May Have Led to Douglas Murder Suicide.

Below the headline, a photograph of her mother and Nicholas Tyson at an outdoor café covered half the page. They sat at a table, beneath a wide umbrella. The likeness between Nick and his father struck her. Same Pacific-blue eyes. Thick brows that gave both men a brooding expression. Strong square jaw.

Something niggled at Sara as she stared at the photo. To the casual observer, they appeared to be friends enjoying a cold drink on a hot day. Upon closer inspection, Sara realized they were looking at an object on the table in front of them.

"What are you doing?" she whispered.

She hit the magnification button. The photo swelled, becoming grainy and losing some detail. But the enlargement was enough for Sara to identify what was on the table in front of them.

A manuscript.

Chapter Five

Darkness had fallen by the time Sara left the library. She'd lost herself in research and somehow spent the entire afternoon reading and printing enough material to keep her busy for a week. The most important thing she'd discovered was the photograph of her mother and Nicholas Tyson looking at the manuscript. Had her mother carried on a relationship with the true-crime writer? Was there, indeed, a missing manuscript?

Sara couldn't get the questions out of her mind as she parked the rental car in the drive. The anonymous caller had mentioned a manuscript. Until this afternoon, she'd dismissed the notion. Now that she'd seen the photo, she wasn't so sure. Nicholas Tyson had been a true-crime writer. He'd written several books, but had never become successful. Had he been working on a book? If so, what was it about? Did the book somehow involve her parents? Did Nick know anything about it? If so, why hadn't he mentioned it when she asked him to reopen the case?

Distant thunder rumbled as she lugged her notebook and oversized purse to the front door and let herself in. Turning on lights as she went, Sara made her way to the kitchen and set her things on the bar. Rain lashed the windows as she traversed the foyer and ascended the stairs. The long and narrow hall stood in darkness. She was midway to her parents' bedroom when it struck her that the bathroom light was on. She was certain she'd turned out the lights before leaving…or had she?

Sara's heart jumped into a fast staccato. Someone was in the house. She hadn't noticed anything out of place downstairs, but she hadn't been paying attention. How did they get in? The front door had been locked. Of course, she hadn't checked the back door….

A clap of thunder made her jump. But the sound was nearly drowned out by the hard pound of her heart. She reached for her cell phone only to realize she'd left it on the counter downstairs. Never taking her eyes from the slash of light beneath the bathroom door, she backed away.

The door swung open. A gasp escaped her when the dark figure of a man emerged. She got the impression of a rail-thin frame and a baseball cap before the flight instinct kicked in and sent her to the stairs. She was halfway down when recognition stopped her. Gripping the mahogany banister, she halted and looked back. A man with silver, shoulder-length hair stood in the hall, looking down at her. He wore gray coveralls, a cap and work boots. She knew his face. His clothes. She knew the way he moved.

"Skeeter?" she ventured in a shaky voice.

The caretaker grinned, his head bobbing vigorously. With the grace of a mime, he stepped back and motioned toward the bathroom. With deft hands he signed something to her. Sara didn't understand sign language, but knew enough to realize this man didn't mean her harm.

Feeling like a fool, she climbed the steps,

flipped on the hall light and crossed to him. "You scared me."

Skeeter spread his hands and gave her a giant shrug.

"How did you get in?" she asked.

Shoving his hand into the pocket of his coveralls, he pulled out a key ring with a single key.

Sara didn't like the idea of anyone having a key to the house, particularly in light of the anonymous calls and the message that had been written on her windshield. She held out her hand. "Thank you, but I'll take that for now and return it when I leave."

He bobbed his head and dropped the key into her hand.

"What are you doing here?" she asked.

He motioned toward the bathroom.

Only then did Sara relax. "You fixed the leak."

He nodded, pleased she understood.

"Thank you." She extended her hand. "I guess I'm a little jumpy."

His gesture told her not to worry. He shook her hand gently, as if afraid he might break her fingers.

She hadn't seen Skeeter since she was a child. He hadn't changed much in twenty years. He was still tall and wiry and moved with an odd shuffle. He still wore gray coveralls and work boots with his hair pulled back into a ponytail. But it had receded and turned gray. Her parents had hired him as caretaker over twenty years ago. Deaf and mute, he'd frightened Sara as a child. But with a child's open mind, she'd quickly realized the man didn't need a voice to communicate—or to be her friend. Because of his deafness, Skeeter dropped out of school and never received special education for his deafness. But over the years, though he was mostly illiterate, he learned to read lips. In the years she'd known him, he'd fixed swing sets, repaired bicycles and erected a basketball net over the garage. By the time that last summer rolled around, she didn't even notice the strange way he moved or that he couldn't speak.

"I didn't see a car," she said. "How did you get here?"

Using his fingers, Skeeter indicated he had walked.

"So you still live in the cottage?"

He nodded.

The "cottage" was actually a tiny mobile home from the 1960s perched high above the cliffs a mile or so down the beach. Skeeter had lived there alone for as long as Sara could remember.

He signed rapidly, mouthing words and then picked up the toolbox at his side. From his body language, Sara understood he'd finished his work and was leaving. "Can I drop you at the cottage?"

Shaking his head, he headed toward the staircase. Sara trailed him to the kitchen, waving as he went through the back door to the steps that would take him to the narrow beach below.

She'd always liked and enjoyed Skeeter. She'd been happy to see him, pleased to know he was still around. It wasn't until she grabbed her notes off the kitchen counter and looked down at the photo of her mother, Nicholas Tyson and the missing manuscript that she realized his being inside the house also troubled her.

THE PHONE CALLS had worked. After twenty years the girl was back. Better yet, she was doing exactly what he wanted her to do. But she was also doing some things he hadn't anticipated. Like asking questions about that night. Too damn many questions.

He assured himself she couldn't possibly uncover anything that could be dangerous to him. The case was closed. Her parents and Nicholas Tyson were dead and buried right along with all the dark secrets.

There was one element he had to consider. Little Sara Douglas had been there that night. She'd witnessed the shooting. She'd seen the killer. The real question was had she heard the argument? Had her seven-year-old mind understood it? What the hell was he going to do if she started piecing things together?

It was some comfort knowing she couldn't remember. Shortly after the killings, he'd read in the newspaper that she'd been so traumatized by the ordeal that she couldn't remember anything about that night. But he knew from experience that memories had a way of resurfacing at the most inopportune time.

This was definitely an inopportune time.

With Sara Douglas sniffing around, he was going to have to be very careful. He couldn't let her ruin this for him. This was his one and only shot at the big time. He'd worked too hard to get where he was. He'd paid his dues. Paid a lot more than anyone should have to. It finally looked like things were going his way. Like he would get the break he deserved. Success. Recognition. A place in the spotlight.

So long as that bitch Fate didn't go and lay down a wild card. But he had to wonder. Was Sara Douglas a wild card?

For the moment, he needed her. She was the one person who could find what he needed. An item that would catapult his career right to the top. But she was also the only person who threatened his ticket to stardom. His dreams. His future. Everything he'd ever worked for. Everything he deserved.

All he could do was give her some rein. Let her sniff. Let her look. If all went as planned she would find the prize. When she did, he would be there to claim it.

Once that happened, Sara Douglas would

become a liability. She would become more dangerous to him than ever because she wouldn't stop there. Once she found what he needed, he would have to find a way to silence her forever.

SARA HAD KNOWN the mansion well as a child. She and her sister had explored every square inch, no matter how dark or dusty and despite her mother's scolding. Tonight, searching for a manuscript that might not even exist, she felt overwhelmed by the sheer size of the place.

"If I were going to hide something, where would I put it?"

Standing in the foyer, she nibbled on her thumbnail and tried to put herself inside the minds of her parents. Her father had designed and built the house himself. Had he considered a place to hide valuables such as jewelry or important documents or family heirlooms?

Rain slashed at the windows as Sara ascended the narrow and winding stairs to the attic. The old hinges creaked like arthritic bones when she opened the door. The odors of dust and mildew tickled her nose. She flipped the switch, and stark light rained down from a single bare bulb dangling from the ceiling. Her shoes thudded hollowly on the old wood floor as she walked inside.

The attic was relatively small with an A-frame ceiling and a single gable window. Cardboard boxes were stacked neatly against the far wall. Someone had painstakingly packed her parents' things. Perhaps one of her aunts or uncles in the weeks following their deaths. Sara had not only been too young, but also too distraught. She hadn't set foot in the house since that terrible night.

Crossing to the boxes, she went to the nearest one and opened it. Inside, she found clothing. Even after twenty years she thought she caught a whiff of her mother's perfume. The scent brought tears to her eyes. She remembered spending time up here with her mother. Sun streaming through the window. Music floating from the radio. The smell of the sea mingling with the sweet scent of roses....

Shoving the melancholy thoughts aside, Sara closed the box and went to the next one. Inside, she found a few of her old toys, a seashell collection from the beach, and several stuffed animals. Deciding to make a trip to the thrift store in town the next day, she closed the box and started a stack of things she would be donating. The third box contained an ancient-looking reel-to-reel recorder, the kind she and her sister used when they watched Godzilla movies and laughed until they cried.

Smiling, Sara closed the box and shoved it against the wall. The next box held dozens of books, old bills, bank statements and several file folders. She paged through a few of the folders and was about to close the box when a spiral notebook caught her attention. Sliding it from its ancient nest, she opened it and began to read.

Strongly slanted handwriting she didn't recognize covered the first dozen or so pages.

Contact in Santa Monica. Evelyn. Real name? Not sure. May be a prostitute. Photo shoot in Hollywood warehouse. Doesn't know where. No police. She has warrants. Nudes. Hinted that she was in danger. Is she credible?

Arlene in East L.A. Photo shoot in Hollywood warehouse. Brother was the last person to see her. Mother filed a missing persons report with LAPD.

Jenna Sherwood. Roommate claims she went for a photo shoot. A magazine spread. Never returned. Owed roommate money for rent. Roomie thinks she may have skipped town. Did she?

Rachel Garza. Twenty years old. Left behind a one-year-old baby. Her estranged husband believed she was trying to break into acting and/or modeling. Mentioned a job in Hollywood. Significant?

"What on earth?" Sara stared at the words, something dark and disturbing enveloping her like a cloud. It appeared someone was tracking women who'd disappeared. But why? What were the notes doing in her parents' things? And whose handwriting was this?

Setting the notebook aside, she pulled out a brown clasp envelope. Inside, she found several yellowed newspaper stories about young missing women. She checked the names against the ones mentioned in the spiral notebook and found two that matched. Someone was, indeed, researching missing persons cases. But who? And why? What was the notebook doing with her parents' belongings?

She paged through several more files, but found nothing relative. Closing the box, she tucked the notebook and envelope beneath her arm. She was almost to the stairs when the lights flickered and went out.

Alarm skittered through her. But remembering the old fuse box, she felt her nerves settle. There was nothing ominous in the works. Just an old house that hadn't seen maintenance in quite some time. Or maybe the storm had taken out the transformer again.

Eyes wide, she felt her way along the wall toward the stairs. A flash of lightning illuminated the room, telling her she only had a few feet to go. Two steps and she rapped her shin against something hard. The old rocker, she realized. "Damn." Reaching down, she rubbed her shin. When she looked up movement ahead sent her heart into overdrive.

For the span of several heartbeats, she stood frozen, trying to decide if she'd really seen a shadow or if it was a figment of an overactive imagination. Or perhaps the shadows of the tree branches moving outside the window.

Her heart tripped when a floorboard creaked off to her right. "Who's there?" she snapped.

A noise directly behind her spun her around. Sara stared blindly into the darkness, certain there was someone in the attic with her. Her breathing quickened. Her pulse roared in her ears. Backing away from the sound she reached for her cell phone only to realize she'd left it downstairs. Damn. Damn. *Damn!*

"I'm calling the police," she called out. "Right now."

A crash to her right sent her into flight mode. Blind and frightened, she turned and dashed in the general direction of the door. She sensed movement ahead. Heard the shuffle of shoes against the floor. She was nearly there when a large body crashed into her.

The impact sent her reeling. Rough hands yanked the notebook and envelope from her grasp. Sara tried to fight, but her feet tangled and she went down, landing hard on her backside. Half expecting an attack, she scrambled to her feet. Disoriented, she lunged in the general direction of the door only to hear it slam.

Two steps and her hand closed over the knob. Panicked breaths rushing in and out, she twisted it and yanked. But the door refused to open.

Not sure if her attacker was still in the room, Sara fought to open the door, yanking at the knob with both hands. She pounded with her fists. Kicked at the wood, but the lock held firm.

"Help!" she screamed.

The only answer to her pleas was the flicker of lightning outside the window and the echo of thunder in the distance.

NICK KNEW BETTER than to let himself dwell on thoughts of Sara. He sure as hell knew better than to drive out to the old Douglas mansion to see her. He had no good reason to be there. He was off duty, after all. Damn it, he shouldn't be here. But she'd dominated his thoughts since the moment he'd laid eyes on her the day before.

He didn't like it one bit. Didn't like having a monkey on his back, telling him what to do. Since losing his wife, Nancy, in a car accident last year, he'd focused on healing. On moving ahead and getting on with his life. Leaving the grief and that dark place he'd been in in the past.

The last thing he needed in his life was someone to care about. Certainly not a woman. He wasn't interested in dating or a relationship. He simply didn't have the emotional energy. Not that Sara would be interested in him, anyway, he assured himself. Chances were, she had some successful, executive-type boyfriend back in San Diego who showered her with gifts and took her to fancy restaurants.

Once she left, Nick would never see her again. He told himself that's the way he wanted it. He didn't need complications. Healing had been a long and grueling road. Now he needed to stay focused on keeping his life on an even keel.

And one day California was going to fall into the ocean and disappear.

Nick wanted to believe it was the year of celibacy that had him chomping at the bit to see her, his hands itching to touch. He'd only gone on a handful of dates since Nancy's car ran off the coast highway and his own life had crashed and burned right along with hers. He didn't want to feel. Didn't miss women. Or intimacy. He didn't miss sex.

Until now, anyway.

Cursing beneath his breath, he pulled into the driveway of the Douglas place. Drizzle danced in the headlights as the beams played over her rental car. Surprise rippled through him when he noticed the house's windows were dark. Odd, since it was only seven o'clock. Had the power gone out again? He hadn't heard anything on the police radio. Only then did he find himself thinking of the message someone had written on her car window—Curiosity killed the cat.

Grabbing his flashlight, he left the car and started toward the front door. Beyond the junipers, the ocean crashed against the rocky beach below. He stepped onto the porch and knocked twice. Concern rippled through him when no one answered. Knocking one final time, he headed around to the rear of the house. Uneasiness washed over him when he found the back door open several inches.

Nick set his hand on his sidearm and silently entered the house. His flashlight beam played over the kitchen and living areas. He listened, but heard nothing as he moved down the hall. Entering the foyer, he shone the light up the nearest staircase. When he saw no movement, he took the steps two at a time to the top.

He cleared three bedrooms, the bathroom and master suite before noticing that the narrow door at the end of the hall stood ajar. The attic, he thought, and drew his weapon. The door opened to a narrow spiral staircase. At the top, a second door was closed.

His pulse spiked when he heard pounding and a muffled voice.

"Sara!" He rushed the stairs. A dozen scenarios scrolled through his mind, none of them good.

"In here!"

Relief flashed through him at the sound of her voice. He tried the knob, found it locked and put his ear close to the door. "Sara!"

"I'm here! Locked in!"

"Are you all right?"

"I'm fine." But fear laced her voice.

"What happened?"

"Th-there was an intruder. I think he locked me in."

Using the flashlight, he checked the old-fashioned keyhole for a key, but found none. "Where's the key?"

"I don't know."

He ran the beam over the floor. "Do you want me to see if I can find it?"

"Just get the door open. It's pitch-black in here."

"Stand back." He gave her a moment to move, then landed a hard kick near the knob.

Wood cracked. The door swung open and banged against the wall. Before he could bring the beam up, Sara rushed out.

She impacted with him hard enough to make him grunt. He caught a hint of fragrant hair and soft skin and a body vibrating with fear.

He backed up a step. "Whoa." Wrapping his hands around her arms, he slowed her. "Take it easy."

For a moment she trembled against him,

her words rushing out on quick, shallow breaths. "I'm sorry," she said. "I'm just…a little claustrophobic."

"It's all right." Directing the beam between them, he got a look at her face, found her pale, her forehead damp with sweat. "How long have you been in there?"

"I don't know. Maybe twenty minutes."

"You locked yourself in?"

"No way." She shook her head. "Someone was there."

"Who?"

"A man. The lights went out. He came at me, knocked me down."

Fury whipped through him at the thought of some goon knocking her down. "You okay?"

"I'm okay. Just…shaken up."

He trained the beam on the lock, trying not to notice the split wood or the antique knob he'd damaged. It wasn't the kind of lock that could engage on its own. "You're sure someone was in there with you?"

Even in the semidarkness he saw anger flash in her eyes. "Of course, I'm sure, damn it."

"All right." Setting his hands on her shoulders, he backed her to the wall. "Hang tight for a moment while I check it out, okay?"

He felt her shiver. "He's gone."

"Stay put. I'm going to take a look anyway." Giving her shoulder a squeeze, he stepped into the attic. The room was small and dark as a tomb. It took him less than two minutes to ascertain that it was also empty. By the time he'd finished, Sara was back inside.

"There's no one here now."

"Someone was, Nick. Someone turned out the lights. They…took the notebook. Locked me inside."

"What notebook?"

"The one I found. In the box."

He raised his hand as if to touch her, then let it drop. "Okay. Let's go downstairs. Make sure you're all right. Check the fuse box. I need to check the grounds, then we'll call this in and file a report. Okay?"

She nodded.

In the kitchen, he put Sara in a chair and went through the back door. He shone the flashlight beam along the juniper and jagged rocks surrounding the deck. Taking the wooden steps that led to the beach, he stopped halfway down and illuminated the low-growing bushes and rock. There were a hundred places a man could hide around the old house, but Nick saw no one.

Back inside, he found her in the utility room, looking at the fuse box. "There's no one out there."

"I was in the attic for quite some time," she said. "They probably ran out the back door."

"Any idea who it was? Anything familiar about them?"

She shook her head. "All I know is it was a man. Strong. Tall."

"That certainly narrows it down." Brushing her aside, he put the beam on the fuse box. Sure enough the main fuse was un-screwed. "Loose," he said.

"Or someone loosened it."

He tightened the fuse. Sudden light shone down. For a moment, they stood there blinking at each other. He found himself looking into pretty brown eyes wide with the remnants of fear. Her hair was pulled into a ponytail, but several wisps teased her face. Dirt smudged her white T-shirt. He didn't want to see more. Sure as hell didn't want to notice any more detail. But his eyes took on a life of their own and swept down her. He saw the outline of a lacy bra beneath a threadbare T-shirt. A strip of flesh where the T-shirt hem met the waistband of low-rise jeans. Lower, he saw long legs and soft curves encased in denim. Painted toenails peeked out from beneath frayed hems.

Giving himself a hard mental shake, Nick stepped back. "What were you doing up there, anyway?"

"That's what I need to talk to you about." Pursing her lips, she turned and walked into the kitchen.

Nick didn't follow. He stood in the utility room a moment longer, silently reprimanding himself for getting caught up in a moment he had no business getting caught up in. There was no way he was going to let himself get sucked in by her female charms.

Instead of following her into the kitchen, he'd cleared the garage and called a report in to B.J. By the time he met her inside, he felt more in control. She stood at the counter, setting a kettle on the stove.

"Tell me everything," he said.

She turned to him. The fear in her eyes had vanished, replaced by determination. "I found a notebook in the attic."

"What kind of notebook?"

"There were details about missing women inside. Notes, I think."

He considered that a moment. "Your parents?"

"I don't think so. I didn't recognize the handwriting."

"What did the notes say, exactly?"

She relayed snippets of notes and newspaper articles that didn't make much sense. "Any idea what that means?"

"No idea," he said. "It's almost as if someone was doing research on missing persons. Missing women who'd disappeared under mysterious circumstances."

Nick thought the scenario she'd pieced together was a stretch, but he didn't say as much. "Your parents were actors. Your father was a producer. They dealt with writers. Movie scripts."

"This was no script."

"What do you think it was?"

"I don't know. Research, maybe." As if suddenly restless, she strode to the dining room. "I wish I had a better answer."

"Sara, where are you going with this?"

She stopped midway to the patio door. Because the water had begun to boil, Nick removed the kettle from the flame.

The sound of her gasp spun him around. Sara stood frozen in the dining room, staring down at the floor.

"Oh my God," she said.

Nick rushed to her and followed her gaze. The hairs at his nape prickled when he spotted the muddy footsteps leading from the deck into the house.

Chapter Six

"Maybe you ought to sit down and tell me everything. No holding out."

Sara slid into the chair opposite Nick and sighed. "I'm not sure where to start."

"The beginning is usually a pretty good place."

Setting her hands on the table before her, she gathered her thoughts. "Two days ago I received an anonymous phone call telling me my father was not a murderer."

"Was the voice male or female?"

"I don't know. It sounded…electronically altered."

"Those devices can be purchased on the Internet for under a hundred dollars." His expression remained impassive. "Go on."

Quickly, she gave him the details of the

call. "He said there was information that would vindicate my father."

"What information? Did he give details?"

"He wasn't specific."

"How do you know the call wasn't some kind of prank?"

She considered that a moment, trying not to feel foolish. "Gut, mostly." She bit her lip. "He called me again this morning."

"What did he say?"

Sara's heart was pounding when she picked up her cup of coffee and sipped. "He told me I had seen the killer that night."

Something dark flickered in his eyes. "Did you?"

"I honestly don't know."

"But it's possible?"

She nodded. "I've spent years trying to remember everything that happened that night. I went through years of psychotherapy. I even underwent hypnosis."

"To no avail."

"Unfortunately."

"What else did the caller say?"

Sara debated whether to tell him everything. The voice had told her not to trust anyone. But there was something about Nick that made her want to confide in him, trust him.

She set down the cup. "The caller mentioned a manuscript."

"You think the notes you found in the attic have something to do with this missing manuscript?"

"Maybe."

His brows snapped together. "What kind of manuscript?"

"He didn't say." Her gaze latched onto his. "Nick, your father was a true-crime writer."

"He was a plumber who published two true-crime novels, neither of which made much more than a ripple in the publishing world."

Uncle Nicholas, the plumber, had forged an unlikely friendship with her parents, the proverbial Hollywood couple. The memory always made her smile. "He was a nice man."

"A good man."

"You look like him."

One side of his mouth curved. "I get that a lot."

She thought of the notes she'd found in the attic. "Nick, I think the notes may have been his."

"Why would his notes be here? He did most of his writing in the bungalow."

"My parents and your father were friends. Good friends. Maybe he left them here."

"Tell me about the notes."

"I only had a minute or so to look at them before the lights went out." Even now, the memory of that moment made her shudder. "It appeared as if someone had written down the names and circumstances regarding the disappearances of several women."

"Do you recall any of the names?"

The question sparked a memory. "Jenna... something. Sherman. No...Sherwood."

Nick pulled a small spiral pad from his shirt pocket and jotted the name down. "I can run that name through the Missing and Unidentified Persons Unit database and see if anything pops."

Hope coursed through Sara at the thought of information that wasn't based on hearsay or loosely pieced-together theory. "Was your father working on a book at the time of his death?" she asked.

"I don't know." He shrugged. "I was twelve. I was always intrigued by his work, but Mom never talked about him after that night."

"Maybe we could talk to her."

"I think you should stay away from Laurel," he cut in.

Remembering her confrontation with his mother, Sara touched the sore spot on her cheek. "She might be able to shed some light on this."

"Being able and being willing are two different things."

"Maybe if *you* talked to her."

He grimaced, as if the idea left a sour taste in his mouth. "She was never the same after Dad died. She's never talked about it, even when I asked. But I'll give it a shot."

"Thank you. I know that won't be easy for you."

"Or her."

Sara picked up her cup to sip, but the coffee had gone bitter on her tongue. "I went to the library when I was in town earlier."

He shot her a dark look as if knowing she was about to tell him something he didn't want to hear.

Sara didn't care. "The *Cape Darkwood*

Press ran a lot of stories on…the crime after it happened."

"Sensational stories sell newspapers."

"There was a photo in one of the stories of my mother and your father sitting at an outdoor café. To the biased eye, it might have looked like an intimate moment between lovers." She took a deep breath. "The reporter played up that angle. On the table between them, there was a manuscript."

His gaze sharpened on hers. "Based on that photo, you're telling me you think there is, indeed, a missing manuscript?"

"I think it's a possibility we should look into." Realizing what she'd said, Sara amended her statement. "*I* should look into."

"Even if you find the manuscript, what do you expect to accomplish?"

"The caller mentioned a manuscript. Maybe it's tied to the killings." But she knew that wasn't the whole truth. More than anything, Sara wanted to vindicate her father of murder and suicide, her mother of infidelity. "I just want to know what happened that night. I want to know why it happened."

"Look, the police did a thorough investigation. I have access to the reports. I've gone over them a dozen times."

"I'm not suggesting the case was botched."

"You're making it sound like some sort of conspiracy."

"Or maybe someone manipulated the scene."

"Are you intimating that someone killed our parents and made it look like a murder-suicide?"

It sounded crazy, even to her. Like the desperate attempts to salvage the reputation of someone whose name was tainted with unforgivable sin. "I think that's a possibility."

Sighing, he scrubbed a hand over his jaw.

Sara tried to ignore the intimate rasp of callus over whiskers, but didn't quite manage. "What about you? Do you think your father and my mother were…involved?"

Nick looked uncomfortable, then shook his head. "From what I know about my father, it doesn't seem likely. He was a good, honest man. A family man. But he was also human with human weaknesses. From all accounts—"

"And you're all too willing to believe the status quo."

He frowned. "Let's just say I've never been a fan of conspiracy theories."

"Nick, put all of this together and I think the entire case warrants another look."

"On the word of some anonymous caller?"

"There's *something* going on. I don't know what. But *someone* called me. *Someone* left that message on my car window. And *someone* was definitely in the house tonight. Strange that all they took were those notes." She met his gaze. "You're the cop. Tell me that doesn't warrant a little suspicion."

"If you think of it in terms of motive, means and opportunity, the fourth-person theory doesn't hold water. If your father wasn't the shooter and someone orchestrated a cover-up twenty years ago, what was their motive?"

"I don't know, but I've barely begun to dig."

"Who would have a motive for wanting to expose a twenty-year-old crime now?"

"Someone with a conscience?"

"Maybe." But he didn't look convinced.

Restless and frustrated, Sara rose and

carried her cup to the sink. "Why would someone call me? Why bring me back into this after all this time?"

"If there was a fourth person that night, maybe you saw them. Maybe they think you can identify them. Maybe you're a loose end he can't live with anymore."

The words sent a chill all the way to her bones. For the first time since she'd arrived, Sara felt vulnerable. Nick must have noticed because he rose and crossed to her, setting his own cup in the sink. "Look, if you're right and things didn't go down the way the police said they did, maybe this is about silencing the only witness. Have you thought of that?"

She turned to him. "If someone wanted me gone, they've had ample opportunity to do it. That first night, for example. I was here. Alone. Why scrawl some ridiculous message on my car? For God's sake, he was in the house tonight. He could have easily…" To her surprise, she couldn't complete the sentence.

"Killed you?" he finished.

The words turned her blood to ice. But she didn't let herself dwell on the rising tide of fear. She hadn't traveled all the way from San Diego to cower at the first sign of trouble. "So you're admitting there's a possibility that the police were wrong?"

"I'm admitting something you should be admitting to yourself. For whatever reason, someone doesn't want you poking around in this."

"But someone *does*. The caller." She smiled, but it felt brittle on her face. "All the more reason to poke, don't you think?"

"Unless poking gets you into trouble."

But Sara accepted the reality that she was going to have to start thinking about her personal safety. When she'd received the call back in San Diego, the thought that she could be placing herself in danger never crossed her mind. Even the bizarre message written on her car window hadn't been enough to stop her. Tonight, however, being locked in the attic and having the notes stolen practically from her hands had shaken her badly. She wasn't sure what to do about it. The only thing she knew for certain was that she wasn't going to let it stop her from finding out what had really happened to her parents that night.

"What are you going to do to keep yourself safe?"

The question snapped her attention back to Nick. He looked slightly belligerent standing there, his dark eyes probing hers with such intensity that she had to look away.

"I'll keep the doors locked," she said. "I'll stay aware. Keep my cell phone handy. Watch my back."

Lowering his head, he pinched the bridge of his nose. "That's not good enough."

"Look, I realize this isn't an ideal situation—"

"It's a hell of a lot worse than that. For God's sake, someone broke into your house. They accosted you in the attic and stole notes that may or may not have anything to do with any of this. It could have turned out a lot worse."

"If you're suggesting I hightail it back to San Diego with my tail between my legs, you have another thing coming. My father might have been murdered. If that's the case, I owe it to him to clear his name."

"If your father didn't pull the trigger that

night, it means someone in this town is guilty of triple murder."

The words scraped up her spine like a cold fingertip. Nick must have noticed because for an instant, she thought he was going to cross to her, put his arms around her, comfort her. But he didn't. Instead, his gaze hardened. He shook his head as if he were a teacher dealing with an unruly student. "It's not safe for you to stay here by yourself."

"I don't have a choice," she snapped.

"You could check into one of the bed-and-breakfasts in town."

"Nick, I was going to do that. When the trip was still in the planning stage, I went out to the Internet to book reservations. That was when I found out your mother owns both B&Bs. I knew staying there would be…uncomfortable. Now I'm glad I listened to my instincts. In case you haven't noticed, she hates me." Remembering the ugly scene at the antique store, she sighed. "Besides, I'm going to look for the manuscript. If it's here in this house, I'm going to find it."

"That's incredibly irresponsible."

"Or maybe that's just the way it is."

"The manuscript may not even exist! Someone could be pulling your chain. Have you considered that?"

"Nick, I *saw* the manuscript. In the photo. I know it exists."

"That could have been any manuscript."

"Or it could be the key to what happened that night." Sara crossed to the sink and grabbed a towel.

He shook his head as if at wit's end. "I guess it would be way too reasonable to assume I can talk you out of staying up here by yourself."

"That would be correct." Striding to the French doors, she knelt and began to scrub the muddy footprints.

"I guess there's only one way to handle it then."

An odd sense of discomfort washed over her. She glanced at him over her shoulder. "What's that?"

"I'll just have to spend the night with you."

NICK CHIDED himself for volunteering for an assignment that was only going to bring him grief. He knew better than to get involved in some crazy crusade that would garner nothing more than disappointment and would possibly get Sara hurt in the process.

But it wasn't his intellect that had gotten him into a position he didn't want to be in. It was a bad case of neglected hormones that had him jumping into the fire feet first and thinking of the consequences after the fact. Hell of a thing considering he was not in the market for a woman, no matter how damn pretty. If he wasn't careful, he might just get burned.

But Nick had always possessed some misplaced, testosterone-driven need to protect the female species. Even if the female in question didn't want a damn thing to do with him. Sara Douglas with her gypsy eyes, curvy body and misplaced determination was no exception.

"Nick, you don't have to do that."

Her voice pulled him from his thoughts. "Maybe you'd rather take your chances with the guy who roughed you up and stole those notes."

She looked away. "I don't think he was out to hurt me. I think he wanted the notebook."

Annoyed, he turned on her. "You've got to

be kidding. If you'd put up a fight or gotten in his way, he might have gone into a rage and shot you." The mere thought made him grit his teeth. "Are you willing to bet your life on that?"

She met his gaze levelly. "In case you're not reading between the lines here, I need to see this through. Maybe it's not safe. But life's that way sometimes. Damn it, Nick, I can't run away from this."

Angry with himself, angry with her, Nick turned away and paced to the patio door. "Yeah, well, I don't feel like sitting around doing nothing while you get yourself killed."

She crossed to him, her eyes flashing, and planted her finger in his chest. "Don't you dare try to manipulate me by scaring me."

Nick braced, hating it because the reaction was more physical than intellectual. He refused to let his eyes sweep down the front of her. But her scent titillated his nose. The porcelain-white of her skin made his fingers itch to touch. The sheen of moisture on her lips made him hungry to taste her.

As if realizing the moment had turned into something she hadn't expected, Sara stepped back. "I'm going to start looking for that manuscript."

Nick watched her walk away, berating himself for enjoying the view just a little too much. "What the hell are you thinking?" he muttered and followed.

He found her in the formal dining room. Nick could tell by her expression she was remembering.

"I spent a lot of time here when I was a kid," she said. "My mom and dad liked to cook. Lots of fancy meals Sonia and I couldn't pronounce. They loved to entertain. We got in the way a lot, but Mom and Dad seemed to love the chaos."

Not knowing what to say, Nick shifted his weight from one foot to the other. "You miss them."

"Every day." She turned moist, thoughtful eyes on him. "This house used to be so full of life and laughter. It's hard to see it so…empty."

"It's the people who fill up a house."

Turning away, she left the room and went to the foyer. There she stood with her hands on her hips, looking around. "If my father wanted to hide something," she said to herself, "where would he put it?"

Nick trailed her as far as the hall, careful not to get too close. He didn't like the way he was reacting to her. Didn't like the feelings boiling beneath the surface inside him. Or the edgy attraction tugging low in his gut. A moment ago he'd wanted badly to reach out, find a way to comfort her. But he was far too smart, far too cautious to let himself get that close.

"Closet?" he offered. "Built-in safe?"

"He designed and built the house himself. He was creative…"

"Secret panel? Floorboard? Attic? Crawl space?"

A flash of memory blinded Sara for a fraction of a second. She and her sister standing in her father's study. A doll that had lost an eye. Her sister lifting a carved wooden panel for a decent burial.

"The study," she said abruptly.

Without waiting for Nick, Sara jogged down the hall toward the study and flipped on the light. She heard Nick moving behind her, but she didn't turn. The memory hovered on the outskirts of her mind and she was afraid it would slip away at any time.

The room stood barren and somehow lonely. Her eyes were drawn to the floor-to-ceiling bookcases and cabinets her father had built so lovingly. The bookcase section took up the top portion of the wall. The cabinets were located in the bottom half. In between, an eight-inch carved mahogany panel shone with a dark-chocolate patina.

Without speaking, Sara went to the panel. The hidden hinges creaked as she lifted it.

"I'll be damned." Nick knelt beside her. "A hidden shelf."

"I remember now," she said. "Dad had measured the shelves and cabinets incorrectly. When he installed them, they weren't tall enough to reach the ceiling, so he added eight inches of dead space and hid it with a wood panel to make it look nice."

"Makes a pretty good hiding place." He shone his flashlight inside. "Let's see if he put it to use."

Sara craned her head and peered in. The shelf was wide, but shallow. She saw naked wood, rusty nails, cobwebs and dust bunnies.

Before she could reach inside, Nick ran his hand along the length of the shelf.

"There's something here."

Sara choked out a laugh when he pulled out the one-eyed doll. "Misty! I can't believe she's still there."

He smiled at her. "Ugly doll."

"She had a lot of personality."

Grimacing, he ran his hand once again along the shelf. "There's something else."

Sara's heart pounded when the reel-to-reel tape came into view.

"What the hell?" Nick said.

"A tape."

"Looks like eight millimeter."

Her gaze went to his. "There was a reel-to-reel projector in the attic."

He blew dust from the tape. "In that case let's go see what someone left for us."

Chapter Seven

Rain tapped like impatient fingers on the roof as Sara pulled out the old silent movie projector. She wanted to think they would run the reel of film to see her and her sister frolicking on the beach or riding ponies at a nearby stable. She knew it was crazy, but she had a bad feeling about what they would find instead. She couldn't ignore the trepidation twisting her gut into knots.

"Gotta be thirty years old." Taking the projector from her hands, Nick looked around for a relatively clear wall on which to project the reel and proceeded to set it up on an old wooden crate full of 33 rpm albums.

"Any idea what's on the tape?" he asked.

"Your guess is as good as mine."

He must have seen the tension on her face because he paused and gave her his full attention. "What?"

"I know this is going to sound silly, but I have a bad feeling about that tape."

"How so?" His eyes lingered on hers a moment too long before he returned his attention to the reel-to-reel. "You think maybe you've seen it before?"

"I'm not sure." Realizing her hands were knotted in front of her, she concentrated on relaxing them, failed.

"Only one way to find out." Flipping the switch, he stepped back.

A square of light appeared on the wall. Minute scratches and flecks of dust flashed black within the square. Numbers flicked by, seconds counting down from ten to one. An instant later, the image of a young woman lying on what appeared to be a box-spring mattress came into view. Sara squinted at the blurred image, realizing with a terrible sense of foreboding that the woman's hands and feet were lashed to the bed.

"Oh no," she whispered. "My God."

When Nick didn't respond, she risked a

look at him. His eyes were riveted to the scene unfolding before them. The muscles in his jaws were tight. His features were filled with some dreadful anticipation Sara didn't understand.

Terrible realization assailed her. A gasp escaped her when the masked figure of a man entered the room. Sara caught a glimpse of the ivory-handled revolver in his hand. The deadly beauty of it. But her focus was on the young woman. *Please don't let him hurt her,* she thought. But she knew the wish was in vain.

There was no audio, but Sara saw the woman's mouth open in a scream. The gunman aimed the weapon at her, and the woman's eyes went wild with terror. Her body bucked and twisted atop the narrow bed. Sara watched, paralyzed by a fear that ran so deep her bones felt as if they had been filled with mercury. She wanted to run from the room, but wasn't sure her legs could do the job.

The pistol jerked in the man's hand. A white puff of smoke rose from the blue steel of its muzzle. Blood trickled stark and black onto the floor. All Sara could think was that this was not happening. It was all some kind of horrific joke.

A sound that was part sob, part curse, choked from her throat. Her mind reeled with the images her eyes took in. Horror. Blood. Death. The utter darkness of pure evil. What in the name of God had they stumbled upon?

Before she could move or speak, Nick's curse cut through the air. Lunging forward, he slammed his fingers down on the power switch. The projector rattled to a stop.

Sara sat down hard on a nearby storage trunk and put her face in her hands. Her mind whirled to process what she and Nick just witnessed. Disbelief mingled with the remnants of horror and spilled over into a mass of emotions she couldn't begin to sort through.

When she found her voice, she raised her gaze to Nick. "That's the most horrible thing I've ever seen."

He shook his head, his features a mask of revulsion. "Unbelievable."

"What in the name of God was that?"

"They call it snuff. Urban legend mostly.

The FBI has never found one to be authentic." Nick shook his head. "It could be fake. Some amateur photographer or techno geek doing some creative editing."

"It looked real."

Scrubbing his hand over his jaw, he nodded. "Yeah, it did."

For the span of several heartbeats the only sound came from the steady pound of rain against the roof. "These types of films may exist in other countries. But here…"

"Smuggled in?"

"I don't know." His gaze met hers. Within its dark depths, Sara saw the extent of his concern and an even darker worry, and she knew after this, nothing was going to be the same.

Crossing to the reel-to-reel, he switched off the projector light. "I'll seal everything and courier it to the Bureau of Forensic Services Lab in Sacramento first thing in the morning, see if the geeks there can authenticate it. The lab will dust for prints. If they find any, they'll run them through the database. If that son of a bitch is in the system, we'll get him."

"What about the woman?"

"I'll see if the lab can lift a still of her face, put it out over the wire. If we're lucky, we might be able to get an ID."

A disturbing new question struck Sara. "What were my parents doing with that tape?"

"I don't know."

"Do you think it has something to do with their deaths?" Her mind spun out rapid-fire questions. "With the person who called me? The person who stole the notes?"

"I don't know." His expression turned granite-hard. "One thing I do is that this has just turned dangerous."

Her mind was still reeling from the horror of what she'd seen. She couldn't get her brain around the ugliness of it. Couldn't believe it was real. "It's almost as if someone *wanted* me here to find that tape."

"Or else they were looking for it, couldn't locate it and wanted you to do their dirty work for them." He motioned toward the wall where the images had played out. "You can bet whoever made that tape and the guy with the gun don't want to be exposed."

Sara pressed her hand to her stomach. "Where does this leave my investigation?"

His scowl deepened. "I don't know about your so-called investigation, but I'd venture to say it leaves you in danger. If you're smart, you'll pack up and go back to San Diego."

It was Sara's turn to laugh, but there was no humor in the sound that squeezed from her throat. "Surely you don't expect me to walk away from this now? I finally have something to go on."

"What you have is a savage murder on tape, and a killer who probably won't hesitate to do it again to keep his secret safe."

"And what about my parents? My father has been painted as a murderer. My mother an adulteress. Am I supposed to just walk away and let that stand?"

"You're supposed to do the smart thing and let the police handle this."

"The way they handled it twenty years ago."

He pinched the bridge of his nose between his thumb and forefinger. "Sara, come on... You know better."

"Nick, please, I know this could be dangerous. And, yes, I'm frightened. But I can't stick my head in the sand. I need to see this through."

"You can't stay here alone. You're a sitting

duck up here. You're isolated with no way to defend yourself."

"Then help me, damn it!"

He shot her a hard look. "Pack your things. I'm taking you into town to find you a room. I'll talk to my mother. Tell her to back off."

"She hates me. There's no way she's going to give me a room at the B&B."

He raised his hands. "Then at least compromise. Meet me halfway."

"How do you suggest I do that?"

"Stay with me. At the bungalow."

NICK WASN'T SURE why he'd offered up his bungalow. The last thing he wanted was for her to stay with him. He didn't like the way he was reacting to her. Didn't like the feelings she conjured. Or the temptation of having her near.

But it was worse when he considered all the terrible things that could happen to her if she stayed here alone. As a cop, Nick had seen plenty of ugliness over the years, but the images on that tape were worse than all of it combined. There was no way he could walk away from this and keep a clear conscience.

He'd never be able to live with himself if something happened to Sara.

A foot away, she stared at him as if he'd just splashed ice water on her face. "Stay with you? At the bungalow?"

"I know it's small," he began. "But I've got an extra bedroom. You'd be safe there. You're still close enough to the mansion that you can drive over during the day and do what you need to do."

Turning away from him, she strode to the window and looked out at the darkness beyond. Even in profile he could see she was troubled. "Nick, I don't want to intrude."

"Hey, I'd be happy for the company."

She turned to face him. "You're sure?"

Nick struggled not to let his eyes drop to take in the length of her. "As long as you don't snore."

"I don't."

Something went soft in his chest when she smiled. Against his better judgment, he smiled back. It had been a long time since he'd experienced this level of affection for a woman. Not since his late wife. There was a part of him that wanted to believe his burgeoning feelings for Sara were a good thing. A sure indication that he was healing.

But after losing Nancy, he'd sworn he'd never care for another human being the way he'd cared for her. Life was too precarious. One minute the woman you loved could be in your arms, the next she could be lying alongside the road dead. Nick had no intention of ever having his heart ripped from his chest that way ever again.

He told himself that wouldn't be a problem. He'd learned to be cautious. He'd had the chance to begin several relationships in the last year, but all of them had ended badly. *Because you sabotaged them,* a little voice reminded. Only later did he realize he'd only been going through the motions. The truth of the matter was he'd never let himself get too close. Never even had sex. Some shrink would probably call it fear of intimacy. Nick figured he was just playing it safe.

There was nothing safe about Sara. She was different. For the first time since Nancy's death, he wanted more. More than was wise. More than he could ever allow.

Realizing he was staring at her, he put the reel-to-reel projector in a large plastic bag and sealed it with boxing tape. "Let me get this processed and we'll go."

Nick removed the reels and sealed them in a separate bag. He gave his work only half of his attention. The other half was on Sara as she wandered the attic, looking in boxes, checking floorboards and any dark niche someone might use as a hiding place.

It was nearly midnight when he piled everything into a beat-up cardboard box and the two of them carried it down the stairs.

Rain fell in sheets as Nick carted the box to his vehicle and shoved it into the trunk. Out of the corner of his eye he spotted Sara lugging her suitcase down the sidewalk. The damn thing was almost as big as she was. Crossing to her, he commandeered it. "Get in!" he shouted to be heard above the rain.

"I need my own car."

"Sara…"

But she was already digging for her keys and walking away.

Shaking his head, Nick watched her get into her car and waited for her to start the engine. Starting his own vehicle, he pulled from the driveway and onto the coast road.

He should have been concentrating on his driving. But by the time he hit the speed limit, the only thing Nick could focus on was the headlight glare of the car behind him, the memory of Sara's sultry perfume, and the knowledge she would be spending the night with him.

One night, he promised himself. Tomorrow, he would make sure she checked in to one of the bed and breakfasts in town for safekeeping. There was no way he was going to risk spending the night with a woman he couldn't keep his eyes off of no matter how hard he tried.

NICK'S BUNGALOW sat at the end of a long narrow lane shrouded with trees and fog. The rain had slowed to a drizzle by the time he parked adjacent to the garage. Sara disembarked, the earthy scents of wet foliage, rich earth and clean air filling her lungs. Because of the dark she couldn't see much of the house itself. Just that it was a small one-story structure with cedar siding and a river-rock chimney. Mullioned windows looked out over the woods. The front porch was made for sitting.

"This is a beautiful location." She lugged her suitcase from the trunk.

"I like the privacy." But his smile looked tight and uncomfortable on his face. "Wait till you see it in the daylight."

He carried the box containing the projector and tapes to the front door, unlocked it and turned on the light. Sara rolled her suitcase inside and was immediately taken aback by the rustic charm of the room. Huge cedar beams ran the length of the ceiling. A colorful Native American print rug covered glossy oak floors. An overstuffed sofa in hues of turquoise, yellow and beige blended nicely with the adobe-textured walls. But it was the river-rock hearth that dominated the room and drew the eye.

"It's lovely, Nick."

"A little messy. I wasn't expecting company."

Two thick novels lay face down in front of the fireplace. A reader, Sara thought, and smiled. Several fringed pillows lay on the floor. A soda can sat on a coaster on a rough-pine coffee table.

"How long have you lived here?"

"Almost two years."

"You live alone?" Sara wanted to believe it was an innocent question. But it wasn't entirely. A small part of her was curious about this man—and wanted to know if there was a woman in his life. Not because she was interested in anything more than friendship, she assured herself, but because Nick was an old friend and she wanted to get caught up on what was going on in his life.

"Just Homer and me."

"Homer?"

"I'm sure he'll come skulking in as soon as he's figured out you're not going to pick him up and squeeze him."

Sara laughed outright, surprised she could do so after the film they'd seen earlier. "I take it Homer is a cat?"

Nick grinned. "Don't tell him that."

As if on cue a large orange tabby shot out of the kitchen and began rubbing against Nick's denim-clad legs. "Don't let him bully you into petting him."

"I love cats."

"In that case." Bending, Nick scooped up the cat and passed him to Sara. "I'll put your suitcase in the extra bedroom."

The cat purred like a small motor in her arms. She'd never imagined a tough guy like Nick Tyson with a cat. While he took her suitcase down the hall Sara strolled to a wall covered with framed photos. Nick with two men, all three of them shirtless and holding beers. In the background, the bungalow was in the throes of remodeling. Below, a shot of Nick with his mother. Nick in full uniform in front of a classroom full of kindergarten-age children.

Sara found her eye drawn to a photo of Nick with a woman. A blonde with mischievous eyes and a laughing mouth. They were close, wearing cutoff jeans and T-shirts. Nick's arm was draped companionably over her shoulder. He was looking into her eyes, smiling as if she were the only woman in the world.

His late wife, she realized. Her sister, Sonia, had kept in touch with one of her friends here in Cape Darkwood and told her about the car accident that had stolen her life. Sara felt a belated twinge of guilt for not calling him to offer condolences, but by then she and Nick had lost touch.

She stared at the photo, the intensity in Nick's eyes, and found herself wondering what it would be like for him to look at her that way....

"Looks like the rain is here to stay."

Startled, Sara spun, only then noticing the din of rain on the roof.

"I didn't mean to scare you."

"I guess I'm still a little jumpy after seeing the tape."

He grimaced. "I hope the lab will be able to glean enough information to help us."

"I just can't figure why my parents had something like that in their possession."

"Richard Douglas was a movie producer." Nick shrugged. "Maybe some crackpot sent it to him."

"Dad wouldn't have kept something like that. He would have sent it to the police."

"You're probably right."

Troubled by the questions pelting her, Sara set the cat on the floor. "Do you think the tape has something to do with their deaths?"

Nick studied her for a moment, his eyes thoughtful. "I'm not convinced their deaths didn't happen exactly the way the police said they did."

Frustration rolled through her. That wasn't what she wanted to hear. It wasn't what she needed to hear. She needed Nick to believe her.

"Then why would someone call me out of the blue and state otherwise?"

"I can't explain that."

"Why won't you at least consider it?"

When she started to turn away, he reached out and touched her arm. "I'm trying to be objective, keep an open mind." He squeezed gently. "Okay?"

She nodded, then watched as he crossed to the dining-room table and switched on his laptop. She joined him as he brought up a law-enforcement site and typed in his ID and password. "What are you doing?"

"The State of California Department of Justice has a Missing and Unidentified Persons Unit. I thought I'd run the name Jenna Sherwood through and see what happens."

"See if she's missing?"

Nick nodded as his fingers played over the keys. "Hopefully, we'll know something in a day or two."

The name made her think of the film. "Do you think the person who was in the house tonight was looking for that tape?"

"It's possible. Likely, even." His brows drew together. "I'm trying to figure out how all of this ties together. The anonymous phone calls. A missing manuscript that may or may not exist. The intruder who stole the notes from you. And now the film."

Sara considered his words, a chill rushing over her. "A book," she said abruptly.

"What book?"

"What if your father was working on a book? Another true-crime novel? What if those notes were his?"

Nick nodded. "That fits. But it doesn't explain the tape."

"Maybe someone involved with the making of that tape had an attack of conscience and sent it to him to expose whomever was responsible. Or maybe they sent it to him to prove this snuff thing was really happening. Maybe your father was investigating." Energized by the emergence of a theory, albeit a dark one, Sara began to pace. "It fits."

"It doesn't explain why your parents were killed."

"Maybe they were in the wrong place at the wrong time."

"Why contact you?"

"Maybe this mystery person wants the whole thing exposed."

"Or maybe it's like I said earlier and they want the last loose end tied up once and for all."

Sara jumped with a loud crash of thunder. Embarrassed, she forced a laugh, but it was a tight, uncomfortable sound. "You really know how to make a girl feel safe."

"False sense of security gets people killed."

Because the words frightened her more than she wanted him to see, Sara turned away and pretended to study the photos, trying to get her heart rate down.

"I'm not trying to scare you," he said after a moment.

"You're doing a good job of it." Gathering

herself, she turned to face him. "But in case you haven't figured it out yet, it's not going to stop me."

He didn't look happy about it. Too bad, Sara thought. She liked Nick. As a person. A man. She liked the memory of him. But she didn't need a man telling her what to do. Even if he thought it was for her own good.

Sara was acutely aware of Nick behind her. He stood so close she could smell the piney-woods scent of his aftershave. She knew it was crazy to be thinking of him in those terms, especially when he didn't approve of what she had come here to do. But she could no longer deny the low-grade attraction that had been simmering between them since the night he'd walked into the mansion.

"It's late," she said. "I should probably call it a night."

He stepped back, putting some much-needed distance between them. "I put your suitcase in the guest room at the end of the hall."

"Thank you," she said. "For being there tonight. For letting me stay here."

"Stay as long as you want."

Feeling awkward and unsettled, she turned away and fled to the guest room.

Chapter Eight

Rain poured with the roar of a thousand waterfalls. Seven-year-old Sara huddled beside her mother's body. Giant sobs wracked her. Oh, how she wanted her mommy to wake up and hold her and tell her everything was going to be okay.

But Sara knew the bad man was out there. On the balcony. With a gun. Covering her face with her hands, she pressed against her mommy's shirt and closed her eyes. The scent of roses and baby powder, the lingering warmth, chased away the terror.

A gust of wind made her lift her head. A fresh wave of horror enveloped her when the man walked into the room. Water dripped from his raincoat onto the floor. Behind him the curtains billowed wildly.

A whimper escaped Sara when she saw the gun. Horror transformed into wild panic when he raised the weapon and aimed it at her face. She cried harder. Great, shaking sobs tearing from her throat.

"Mommy. Wake up. Mommy!"

The bad man wiped his face with his sleeve. "Sorry, kid," he whispered.

Sara saw tears in the man's eyes, and for a crazy moment she wanted to run to him, throw her arms around his hips, beg him to stop. But she was too afraid to move.

She closed her eyes.

The ensuing gunshot rocked her brain.

And Sara began to scream.

"Easy. Whoa. It's me."

The familiar voice pried into her consciousness. Strong hands gripped her shoulders. Disoriented, Sara brushed at the hands, tried to twist away. All she could think was that the man with the gun was in the room, that she and her family were in danger.

"Sara. It's Nick. You're okay."

Recognition cut through the fog of terror. Sara blinked him into focus. His face registered. Strong features and concerned eyes.

His hands firmly but gently squeezing her shoulders. The fear receded back into its deep, dark hole.

She knew it was silly, but she looked toward the window, almost expecting to see the man with the gun. The nightmare had been so terribly real….

"You cried out in your sleep." Nick tilted his head as if to get a better look at her. "You okay?"

Sara tried to smile, but it felt phony on her face. "Yeah, just…embarrassed."

"Don't be." He grimaced. "That film was pretty hard to stomach."

Only then did she realize he thought the tape had given her nightmares. "It wasn't about the film."

"Then what?"

"I dreamed about the night my parents were killed."

His eyes burned into hers. "Did you remember something?"

She shook her head. "I don't know. It's almost as if…after all these years my subconscious is trying to tell me I saw more that night than I ever realized."

"More than you were able to tell the police," he finished.

She nodded. "It's hard to tell how much of the nightmare is from the power of suggestion and how much of it might be a true memory trying to surface."

"You want badly to exonerate your father."

"Yes, I do. That's why I don't trust this."

He nodded as if he understood. "What do you see in the dream?"

"I'm there. In my parents' room. My mother is on the floor. I'm huddled against her. When I look up there's a man in a raincoat standing on the balcony. He has a gun." A tremor rippled through her at the memory. "I'm terrified. I look at him. I think he's crying. He raises the gun, points it at me. I close my eyes. The gunshot sounds like a crack of thunder." She shook her head. "It always ends the same way."

"Do you recognize the man?"

"No." But something pinged in the back of her mind. Sara raised her gaze to Nick's. "But I think I may have seen him before."

"You mean recently? Or as a child?"

"As a child. My God."

"A friend of your parents? Who?"

Rubbing at her temples, she wracked her brain. "I don't know."

For several minutes she focused every ounce of energy on remembering. But her mind refused to open those doors to the past. Slowly, she became aware of Nick's proximity. She was sitting propped against her pillows. He sat next to her, so close their bodies touched. His arm wasn't quite around her, but rested protectively over her shoulder.

Sara knew it was crazy to be thinking of how solid he felt against her when she should be focused on prying the memories from her head. But there was no way she could ignore the butterflies that had taken flight in her stomach or the hard pound of her heart against her ribs. She was honest enough to admit neither had anything to do with the nightmare—and everything to do with the man.

"Sometimes memories emerge in their own time frame," he said after a moment. "You can't rush them."

The words were thick, his voice deep and rough. Sara knew better than to look at him. But then she'd always been drawn to danger.

She risked a glance to find his eyes already on hers.

"I don't know if these are memories, Nick. I don't know if these dreams are something my subconscious has manufactured because I want so badly to exonerate my father."

"The mind is a powerful thing," he said slowly.

"Especially when you combine it with the heart."

She knew he was going to kiss her. Just as she knew it would be smarter for her to turn away. To slide from the bed. Leave the room. Pretend nothing had happened. The timing was all wrong. Neither of them were looking for a relationship. She wasn't sure she wanted to spoil the tentative friendship they'd formed in the last days.

But the pull to him was as powerful as the storm-driven waves that crashed incessantly against the beach. She made a half-hearted attempt to avert her face. But he caught her chin with his fingertips and turned her face to his.

His mouth brushed hers with the gentle touch of a feather. The contact was light, hesitant, but Sara felt it deep inside. She fought the slow wave of pleasure that engulfed her. She didn't want Nick's kiss to sweep her away. But her will was no match for the electric spark that burned low and hot in her belly.

The sound of protest died on her tongue. When she opened her mouth to stop the temporary madness, the only sound that emerged was a sigh. It reverberated through her entire body. And while her heart beat with a rapid-fire tempo, her muscles turned to jelly.

The next thing she knew, Nick's hand was at her nape, tilting her head back. His kiss turned voracious, and he ravaged her mouth with his. Sara knew she should not let this continue. She should not let herself get side-tracked or give Nick the wrong impression.

But his kiss made the world tilt beneath her feet. It made her blood run hot, her body burn until she thought her skin would melt. She kissed him back with a ravenous hunger she'd never before experienced. It rampaged through her body, a crazed beast running out of control with its first heady taste of freedom.

Her every sense heightened to a fever

pitch. She was keenly aware of his mouth against hers, his kiss firm and demanding. She could feel the scrape of his whiskers against her skin. The warm pressure of his fingertips at her throat. His other hand seemed superheated as it rested against her waist. She sensed the restlessness within him, and she knew if she didn't put a stop to this, those restive hands would begin to roam. It frightened her to think she might not have the intellectual wherewithal to stop.

Sara had never considered herself impulsive or prone to making bad decisions. She'd had relationships in the past, but no man had ever made her ache. In the last two minutes, Nick Tyson had changed everything. If only her heart would stop pounding, she could think long enough to do the right thing and pull away.

Vaguely, she was aware of a crack of thunder outside. The wind rushing through the trees. She could hear Nick breathing hard. But all of it was nearly drowned out by the jackhammer rhythm of her heart. It was too much. Too powerful. Too *breathtaking*. And far too dangerous to continue…

A clever turn of her head and Sara broke the kiss. Nick's face lingered close to hers for the span of a heartbeat, then he pulled back and sat up.

"I'm sorry." His voice grated like rusty steel.

Sara couldn't meet his gaze. Her body still vibrated with the remnants of his kiss. "It's okay," she said. "I just...I was..." For the life of her she couldn't think of how to end the sentence.

"Caught up in the moment," he finished.

"Something like that." Their gazes clashed, held. Heat simmered within his. Electricity seemed to arc between them. He was still sitting on the bed. Too close. There was too much heat between them. Too much temptation zinging back and forth.

As if realizing they were about to repeat a mistake that never should have happened in the first place, he rose abruptly. "I didn't mean for that to happen. I'm sorry. I was out of line."

"Me, too."

Nick paced to the door, then turned to look at her. "You going to be okay?"

Sara tugged the blanket up to her chin. "I'm going to be just fine."

His gaze lingered an instant longer. Then without another word, he opened the door and walked out.

NICK LAY in the darkness and listened to the storm, trying in vain not to think of Sara sleeping in the next room. What the hell had he been thinking? Marching in there when she'd been in the throes of a nightmare and kissing her? The truth of the matter was he hadn't been thinking at all. At least not with his head.

"Idiot," he muttered.

The alarm clock on the night table told him it was almost 4:00 a.m., but Nick knew sleep would not come again tonight. He told himself he was merely worried about the film they'd found. But he was a cop and an experienced one; he didn't get overly keyed up over the job anymore.

He didn't want to admit that he was a hell of a lot more wound up over Sara than he was the film.

What the hell had he been thinking?

"You weren't, buddy," he muttered.

He wanted to blame his sudden case of

lust on a year of celibacy. On the fact that he was finally healing. That he was ready to move on with his life. He wanted to believe he would have acted the same way with any pretty female. But it was a flimsy lie. Sara Douglas wasn't just any woman. Nick knew it sounded ridiculous, but he'd been half in love with her since he was a kid. Could those kinds of immature feelings survive two decades? Could they survive adolescence and maturity? Marriage and the black grief of losing the love of your life?

Nick didn't want to believe so. He didn't want to have any complicated feelings for Sara. He much preferred even keel over powerful and complex. But after touching her, after kissing her, he knew there would be no going back to the way things were before.

Troubled by the reality of that, he threw his legs over the side of the bed and put his face in his hands. He was going to have to keep his distance. That would be difficult with her back in town and digging into a twenty-year-old murder mystery. Even more difficult knowing she was in danger. Could he keep her safe and still keep his distance?

Walking into the bathroom, he twisted the shower knob, going heavy on the cold and tried not to think about Sara Douglas or the turn of events that had put her in danger. Nick had done all he could to keep her safe. He'd offered her refuge at his home.

Now, it was up to Sara to do the smart thing by backing off and letting the police handle the rest.

Chapter Nine

The mansion was perched on the cliffs like an elegant cat, Sara thought as she pulled into the driveway and killed the engine. Nick had already been gone when she'd wakened an hour earlier. There was no note telling her where to find coffee or when he would return. There was no scribbled apology for what had happened the night before.

Sara wanted to be annoyed. But she knew the kiss they'd shared was not his fault. Nick might have instigated it, but she hadn't stopped him. In fact, she'd been as into it as he was. That made her every bit as guilty as him.

Even now the memory of the kiss made her heart quicken. She could still feel the insistent pressure of his lips against hers. The warm brush of his breath against her face. The scrape of his whiskers against her cheek. Her traitorous body responding in a way that shocked and embarrassed her.

"Enough, already," she muttered, pulling out her key and unlocking the front door.

The smells of dust and stale air met her when she stepped inside. She tried not to think of the intruder from the night before as she walked from room to room, making sure no one had broken in during the night. She checked the garage and the patio doors and found both secure.

Nick told her not to come here alone. But Sara had never been good at taking orders. There was no way she could sit around the bungalow and do nothing until he came home from work. It was daylight, after all. The doors and windows were locked down tight. She had her cell phone handy. If someone pulled into the driveway or knocked on the door or even broke a window, she would have ample time to take evasive action.

Still, her nerves were on edge as she wandered to the kitchen and put the kettle on the flame. An ocean gale lashed at the window above the sink as she waited for the water to boil. A few minutes later, steaming coffee mug in hand, she wandered to her father's study and looked around. Richard Douglas had spent much of his time here, sitting at his desk with the phone in the crook of his neck. A good bit of that time had been shared with Sara's mother and Nicholas Tyson.

Setting the cup on one of the built-in bookcase shelves, Sara ran her fingers along the intricately carved wood. She told herself she wasn't looking for a secret compartment. That would be far too…hokey. But Sara knew that when her father had designed the house, he'd made a few architectural errors and corrected them by indulging in a hiding place or two. She felt silly looking, but what would it hurt?

Two hours later she stood at the patio door and watched rain stream down the panes. All she had to show for her time so far was a caffeine buzz and dusty hands. But, for better or worse, Sara had never been easily deterred.

She was on the staircase heading toward the second level when her cell phone chirped. Her heart went into overdrive when she looked down and saw Nick's name come up. The urge to answer was strong, but she resisted. She knew he wouldn't be happy about her coming here alone; she didn't feel up to defending herself. Besides, after what had happened between them last night, better to let things cool off anyway.

Methodically, Sara searched each room. Frustration lay thick in the pit of her stomach when she found nothing of interest. She was thinking about calling it a day when she found herself looking at the attic door. She didn't want to go up those stairs, particularly after what had happened the last time. After seeing that terrible film. But even more, she didn't want to walk away empty-handed.

"Just a quick look-see, Douglas," she muttered as she opened the door and started up the narrow staircase.

The attic was just as she and Nick had left it. The memory of the film flashed vividly in her mind. For the life of her she couldn't figure out why her parents had had it in their possession. A part of her hoped Nick would come back with proof that the murder depicted in the film wasn't real. But deep inside she knew it was. Something so horrific, so ugly, would be difficult to reproduce with such awful authenticity.

She started at the shelves above the window that looked out over the rocky cliffs and churning ocean below. Leaving no place untouched, she lost herself in the search for something—*anything*—that would answer her questions and, she hoped, clear her father's name.

An hour later the attic still had not given up the secrets her parents had taken with them to their graves. Facing defeat and the disappointing notion that the anonymous caller was, indeed, a crank, Sara stepped back from her work and sighed.

Hands on her hips, she stood near the window and looked around. "Damn it."

For the first time, she seriously contemplated the reality that her trip to Cape Darkwood would net nothing. That she would not be able to clear her father's name. That, perhaps, the events of that terrible night twenty years ago had gone down exactly as the police had surmised. There was nothing left to do but lock up the house and head back to Nick's.

With a heavy heart, Sara left the attic and trudged down the staircase. In the hall, she passed her father's study, but instead of going to the kitchen for her purse and keys, she found herself drawn into the room. For an instant she was seven years old again. Her mother was curled on the settee in front of the window with a martini in her hand. Her father sat at the desk, his tortoiseshell glasses pushed onto his head. Across from him, Nicholas Tyson sat in a tapestry wingback chair, smoking a fragrant cigar. Her father's study had been a place for adult work and conversation. A place for important phone calls, computer work and, many times, laughter. It had been one of her favorite rooms in the house.

She wandered the room, feeling foolishly melancholy, touching the shelves as she passed the built-in bookcases. It was times like this when she wondered what her life would have been like if her parents hadn't died on that terrible night. She and Sonia had been blessed with fabulous parents. Still, she couldn't help but wonder.

At the hearth, she ran her hands along the walnut mantelpiece, admiring the work-manship. She was almost to the window when something out of place snagged her attention. Backing up a step, she squinted at the intricately carved wood, trying to figure out what wasn't quite right about it. Her gaze landed on a side piece that connected the mantel to the wall. It was almost as if the wood had been improperly cut and didn't fit well....

Sara reached out and tugged. The panel came easily away, revealing a small space between the wall and the stone hearth. Her pulse kicked when she spotted the tapestry journal hidden inside.

"What in the world?"

Reaching into the small space, she pulled it out. The cover had once been gold with embossed red roses, but time and dust had dulled both. She blew lightly and dust motes erupted. Her hands shook when she opened the journal to the first page. She realized immediately the strongly slanted handwriting was the same as the notes she'd found in the attic. Not her parents'. But whose?

She skimmed through several pages. Her heart beat like a jackhammer in her chest when she realized some of the passages were nearly identical to the ones she'd read in the notes that had been stolen from her the day before. Missing women. Details about their lives carefully documented.

By whom? she wondered. *And why?*

Realizing she needed to sit down and read the journal from cover to cover, she closed it, replaced the panel and headed for the kitchen for her purse and keys. She would do her reading at Nick's where she was certain no one would accost her and steal what she had found.

Snagging her purse from the counter, she dropped the journal inside and headed for the door, digging for her keys as she went. She was midway there when through the side-light, movement in the driveway caught her eye. Her first thought was that Nick had stopped by to berate her for coming here alone. But when she peered through the beveled glass, she saw a figure in a dark raincoat standing next to her car.

Sara pulled her cell phone from her purse and punched in Nick's number. When his voice mail picked up, she left a hurried message then opened the door and stepped furtively onto the porch.

The hooded figure glanced her way and she caught a glimpse of the pale oval of a face. But in a flash he was gone, ducking around the house and disappearing into the drizzle and mist.

Sara paused long enough to utter a mental warning to herself. Looping the strap of her purse over her shoulder, she dashed from the house and ran toward her car. Her breath caught in her throat when she spotted the red lettering on the driver's window:

You don't belong here.

It was anger that struck her this time. Not giving herself time to debate, she set off at a dead run after the culprit. Intellectually, she knew running after a potentially dangerous man was a crazy thing to do. But she was tired of the threats. Tired of letting him yank her chain. And damn tired of being frightened. As she tore around the side of the house, she rationalized that if he had truly wanted to hurt her, he'd had ample opportunity.

She clung to that thought as she blew by the deck at the rear. She started toward the stairs that would take her to the beach, but spotted footprints in the sandy soil leading north, parallel with the beach. A split second decision and she was running along the rocks.

Toward Skeeter's cottage, a little voice whispered.

She didn't want to believe that. Skeeter was strange, but she'd adored him since she'd been a child. But the more rational side of her brain reminded her that sometimes even good people did bad things if pushed far enough.

Wind from the sea tore at her face and clothes as she ran. Icy rain soaked her clothes. But Sara didn't stop. She didn't know what she was going to do if she caught up. Get a look at his face so she could identify him for the police. She didn't think beyond that.

Two hundred yards from the house, the land dropped away into a narrow gorge that caught rain and fed it to the ocean. Standing on the brink, she caught a glimpse of the dark raincoat midway to the ravine floor.

"Stop!" she shouted.

The man glanced back, but didn't stop. Why is he running? Why not stop and make a stand? The questions propelled her forward. She went into the ravine at a dangerous speed, her shoes slipping on moss-covered rocks and sliding in mud. Somehow she managed to maintain her footing.

The trees seemed to swallow her, engulfing her in shadows. Pausing at the foot of the ravine, she looked around, caught a glimpse of the dark figure struggling up the other side. "Wait!" Sara shouted. "I want to talk to you!"

The figure continued climbing up the steep slope. Sara sprinted after him, negotiating around trees and rocks the size of small cars. At the rim, she paused, breathless, the muscles in her legs burning.

Rain slashed down from a slate sky. To her left, at the bottom of the rocky cliff, the ocean roiled and churned. Wiping wet hair from her eyes, she started toward the rocks for a better vantage point. She used her hands and climbed to the top. For an instant, the view took her breath away. Even frightened and soaked to the skin, she couldn't help but marvel at the hostile beauty of the sea and the violence with which it met the land.

She was in the process of reaching for her cell phone to call Nick again when movement from directly behind her spun her around. Too late she realized her mistake. She caught a glimpse of a dark raincoat, shiny and wet. The figure launched at her. Sara knew what he was going to do and tried to drop to the ground to avoid it. But she wasn't fast enough. He hit her with both hands hard enough to knock the breath from her lungs.

A scream tore from her throat.

And then she was falling into space....

NICK DIALED Sara's number for the third time and cursed when she didn't answer. She'd sounded frightened in her message. *I'm at the house. There's someone here. Gotta go. I'll call you right back.*

Her words had lodged a chill at the base of his spine.

What the hell was she thinking, going to the house alone after everything that had happened? Damn crazy woman.

His cruiser slid sideways as he sped into the driveway. He stopped behind her rental car and slammed it into gear. Shoving open the door, he hit the ground running.

He saw something scrawled in red on her driver's-side window. The letters were nearly washed away by the rain, but he was able to make out the words:

You don't belong here.

He sprinted to the front door. A layer of cold fear settled over him when he found it ajar. Bursting inside, he stopped in the foyer. "Sara!"

He ran to the kitchen, shouting her name. He couldn't help but think this house had seen more than its share of death. In his mind's eye, he saw her sprawled on the floor in a pool of blood, the way she'd found her parents. The ensuing rush of terror nearly paralyzed him.

Spinning away from the kitchen, he dashed down the hall and took the steps two at a time to the top. "Sara! Damn it, answer me!"

The fear was making him angry. Angry at Sara for being so irresponsible. Angry at the son of a bitch who'd targeted her. Nick checked the rooms, but knew he wouldn't find her. The house was empty. Where the hell had she gone?

Frantic now, he stumbled down the steps and ran out the front door. He warned himself to stay calm. As a cop he knew a cool head was his best tool in a situation like this.

But this was personal. And in that moment the fear had a death grip on his throat. For the span of several rapid-fire heartbeats, he stood in the driveway, barely noticing the rain soaking him. Where the hell was she?

"Sara!"

He glanced toward the side of the house. His pulse redlined when he noticed footprints in the wet grass and sand. There was no way old footprints could survive days of rain. They had to be fresh.

Nick raced to the tracks and followed them north, toward the gully-washer that ran from the road and emptied into the ocean. All the while, his mind conjured images of all the terrible things he might find.

"Sara! Where are you?"

The prints led him into the ravine and up the other side. Two sets of them, he was sure. Larger ones with a plain sole. And smaller imprints, with a sharper heel. *Sara's,* he thought.

The footprints led to an outcropping of rock on the north rim of the ravine. Nick paused to listen, but heard nothing over the downpour and the crash of the sea. Cupping his hands on either side of his mouth he called out her name.

He was midway down the rock when he heard a cry. A first, Nick thought the sound was a figment of his imagination, brought about by wanting to hear her voice so badly his brain had conjured it. Then he heard it again.

He rushed to the top of the rock and looked around wildly. "Sara!"

"I'm here!"

His stomach dropped when he realized her voice was coming from below. Scrambling to the ledge, he knelt and peered over. His breath jammed in his lungs when he spotted her on a narrow shelf ten feet down. The first thing that registered was that she had blood on her face. A dozen horrible scenarios rushed through his brain. She'd been shot. She'd fallen and struck her head. Then it occurred to him that she was standing, trying to climb back up the face of the rock.

Dangerous, considering that just a few feet from where she stood, the ledge dropped fifty feet to the rocky beach below.

"Don't move," he shouted. "Are you hurt?"

"I'm okay. Just…banged up."

"Stay put. Don't try to climb up. I'll come get you."

"Be careful," she cried. "There's someone else up there. He pushed me."

His sidearm was out of its holster even before she'd completed the sentence. Nick stood, looked uneasily around. The hairs on his nape prickled when he spotted the crude letters scrawled on a rock face ten feet away in dripping red paint. The same type of paint that had been used to write the words on her car window the day before and again today.

Blaine Stocker.

"What the hell?"
Crossing to the rock, he set his finger against the paint—Blaine Stocker.
The name sparked a memory, but he couldn't place it. The only thing he knew for certain was that he'd heard it before. The paint was slowly being washed away by the rain. The cop in him wanted to preserve it for clues, but the man in him wanted only to get Sara off of that ledge.
To do that he needed a rope. Ten feet wasn't that far to pull someone up, but the rocks were slick with moss. If he couldn't find a foothold, pulling her up would be difficult. But Nick didn't want to leave her alone. As far as he knew the bastard who'd pushed her might return to finish the job.

He walked back to the ledge. Setting his gun on the ground, he stretched out on his stomach and reached for her. "Can you reach my hand?"

She tried, but their fingers were several inches apart. "Maybe we can use my purse strap. It's leather."

"That'll work."

Grabbing her bag, Sara stepped up on a small jut of rock, stood on her tiptoes and extended the strap.

Nick scooted dangerously close to the edge and grasped the strap. Her fingertips touched his hand as he twisted it around his fist. She did the same, wrapping the leather strap around her wrist. "Okay, I'm ready."

"Whatever you do, don't let go," he said.

"Like that's an option at this point."

He dug in with his feet as much as he could and began to pull. His muscles quivered with the exertion. Even though he was soaked, sweat broke out on his skin.

"Use your feet to climb," he ground out.

He could hear her choking with effort as she squirmed and pushed her way up the sheer face of rock. Her free hand grasped dry grass next to his shoulder, her fingers digging into mud like claws.

Nick heaved as hard as he could. Her shoulders emerged. He scrambled back, using his weight to pull her full length onto the rock.

Relief made his muscles go slack. For several seconds the only sounds came from their labored breathing and the crash of the surf below.

Because he was angry, Nick didn't go to her right away. Instead, he focused that burst of energy on the person who'd pushed her off the cliff. The thought of someone hurting her—trying to *kill* her—filled him with a cold and dangerous rage. Reaching for his weapon, he rose and scanned the area. He wanted to go in search of the son of a bitch; he wanted to smash his face with his fist. But Nick needed to calm down and make sure she was all right first.

Next to him, Sara struggled to her hands and knees. Her hair hung wetly in her face. Her clothes were soaked and covered with mud. When she looked up at him, the pale cast of her complexion and the blood dripping down her forehead unsettled him.

"Let me help you." Setting his hands beneath her arms, he helped her rise. She was small within his grip, her entire body trembling violently. "Easy does it," he said.

"Did you see anyone?" Her eyes were already scanning the surrounding brush and the shadows within the trees in the ravine.

"No." But that didn't mean there wasn't someone out there, watching them, waiting.

"There was someone here. A man. I—I followed him from the house. He pushed me." Her voice shook, the words tumbling out too fast.

"I'll get a couple of officers out here." He looked at the cut on her forehead and another wave of anger engulfed him. "Right now I need to make sure you're okay."

"I'm fine. I just…I need to know who did this and why."

"Sara, you're cut. Let's go inside."

"Oh my God." She gaped at the last remnants of the name someone had painted in red on the rock. "I know that name."

"How so?"

"I'm not sure, but I've heard it."

"It's familiar to me, too. But we'll have to

figure it out later. For now we need to get you inside. That cut looks nasty."

When she balked, he took her hand and gently tugged her in the direction of the house.

He led her back into the ravine and up the other side. All the while, he kept his eyes on the surrounding underbrush. The line of trees to the east. The thought that someone had tried to kill her never left his mind.

Once inside, Nick locked the door behind them and headed toward the kitchen. Only then did he realize he was shaking nearly as badly as she was. He wanted to blame it on adrenaline or anger or the physical exertion of his sprint into the ravine. But he knew his pounding heart and shaking hands had more to do with Sara and how close she'd come to being seriously hurt—or worse.

Not wanting to examine that too closely, he walked to the sink and ran water from the tap into a glass. He turned to hand it to her, only to find her at the patio door, looking out.

Frowning, he approached her and handed her the glass. "Do you have any idea how crazy it was for you to come here alone?"

"I know. It was stupid. I'm sorry." Her hand shook when she accepted the glass. "I guess I didn't think the situation would escalate to something like this."

"Most people don't expect to become crime victims." The words came out more angrily than he had intended. He couldn't help it. Her coming here alone had been worse than foolhardy. "Damn it, Sara, it could have turned out a hell of a lot worse."

"It didn't." She touched the cut on her forehead, and he shook his head in disbelief.

Because he was dangerously close to losing his temper, he tugged his cell phone from his belt and dialed the police station. B.J. answered on the first ring. "Hey, Chief."

"I'm out at the old Douglas place. A prowler assaulted Ms. Douglas. I need an officer." A K-9 unit would have been helpful, but it wasn't in the Cape Darkwood budget, so he had to settle for a single officer.

"Damn, Chief. Is she okay?"

He scowled at Sara. "She's fine, but the guy nearly pushed her off the cliff."

B.J. whistled. "I'll dispatch Sammy right away."

Nick thanked him and disconnected. Now that his nerves had settled and the initial burst of fear had ebbed, a controlled anger was setting in. He looked around for a place for her to sit and some decent light so he could see to the gash on her forehead. Since there wasn't a breakfast table, he crossed to the counter and patted it. "Have a seat and let me take a look at that cut."

She crossed to the counter. "You're angry."

"Damn straight I am." Setting his hands beneath her arms, he lifted her onto it, trying not to notice how good she felt in his arms. He found a kitchen towel hanging by the sink and took it to her. For the first time he got a good look at her face.

"Damn it, Sara."

Her eyes were dark and wide within her pale face. The cut on her forehead oozed blood. A bruise was beginning to form beneath it. Wetting the towel, he dabbed at the cut, hoping the wound wasn't as bad as it looked.

"Were you unconscious at any time?" he asked.

She gave him a half-hearted smile. "I was too scared to pass out."

Nick didn't smile back. "You should go to the emergency room."

"I'm okay."

"What you did was unbelievably foolhardy."

She met his gaze levelly. "Yes, what I did was dumb. I've already admitted that. But put yourself in my shoes."

He was feeling far too hostile to concede to her, so he remained silent.

Her lips turned down into a frown. One glance and Nick found himself thinking of the kiss they'd shared the night before. Before he could stop himself, his gaze dipped lower. To the damp T-shirt and jeans that clung to her like skin. Considering the circumstances, she shouldn't have looked sexy. He shouldn't let himself notice. But he did.

"Don't be angry," she said.

"You scared the hell out of me," he growled.

"I scared the hell out of myself."

Steeling himself against the pull to her, he turned his attention to the wound. "It doesn't look like you need stitches, but you've got one hell of a bump."

"I guess it's a good thing I've got a hard head."

Nick couldn't help it; he smiled. He knew that was what she wanted. To draw him out so he wouldn't berate her for doing something stupid. Usually, he wasn't so pliable, especially when it came to the safety of someone he cared about. But there was something about Sara that made him feel light inside, made him want to smile.

"If I didn't like you so much, I'd give you a good dressing-down."

"You'd probably be wasting your time."

He dabbed at the wound and she winced. "Sorry."

But her mind obviously wasn't on the cut. "We need to find out who Blaine Stocker is."

"We will. Give me a minute here, will you?"

She didn't seem to hear him. "Who would do something like this? What could they possibly have to gain?"

"I don't know," he admitted. "But we need to find out because I'm not going to let the son of a bitch get away with trying to kill you."

Chapter Ten

Nick's officer was gone by the time Sara stepped out of the shower and slipped into dry clothes. She'd thought the hot water would soothe the bruises and aches she'd sustained in the fall. Instead, every insult to her body had come to life with a vengeance.

She started down the stairs to find Nick standing near the front door. He looked up as she descended. "Any sign of the man who pushed me?" she asked.

He shook his head. "Sammy and I set up a grid and searched the area, but we didn't find anything. Most of the footprints were washed away by the rain. Even the writing on your car window is gone." He grimaced. "He's heading over to talk to the caretaker now."

Skeeter, Sara thought, and felt a tinge of

sadness. She didn't think the caretaker was responsible; the man who'd pushed her had seemed much more agile. But she couldn't say for certain. "Did your officer recognize the name Blaine Stocker?"

"He had the same reaction we did. The name seemed familiar, but he couldn't place it. I'll hop on the Internet when we get back to the bungalow." He regarded her, concern evident in his eyes. "How are you feeling?"

"Sort of like I got run over by a stage-coach and a team of mules." She managed a smile.

He didn't smile, but his expression lightened. "You look better."

"Purple becomes me." When he simply stared at her, she pointed to the bruise on her forehead. "That was a joke."

"Not funny." But he finally smiled.

His clothes were still damp. She wished she could offer him something dry to wear, but all she had were the few items she'd left in her closet.

"We need to talk about what happened," he said after a moment. "Then we need to get a few things straight."

"Nick, I'm not in the mood for a lecture—"

"I'm not going to lecture you." Gazing steadily at her, he shifted his weight from one foot to the other. "I think we need to take a long, hard look at everything you've uncovered since you've been here."

Her pulse kicked with anticipation. Sara knew it was a silly reaction, but she also felt grateful that he was finally starting to believe her. "So you think the police may have been wrong?"

"I believe all of this warrants a very careful look." He scowled at her. "By me."

The memory of the journal she found sent her rushing for her bag. "I almost forgot."

"What?"

She tugged the faded tapestry journal from her purse and set it on the table in front of her. "I found this hidden in a compartment in the hearth mantel." Her hand shook when she held it out.

He opened the journal and began to page through it. "That's my father's writing."

"It's the same writing as the notes I found in the attic."

"What the hell are my father's notes

doing at your parents' house?" he wondered aloud.

"Nick, I think maybe they'd been working on something together."

"A book?"

She nodded. "It makes sense."

As if by unspoken agreement, they began to read.

Twenty-two-year-old Helen Murchison went to a photo shoot in Hollywood and never returned. Her roommate, Kim Cable, reported her missing the next morning. No one would have dreamed her torn and battered body would be found a week later in a dry riverbed in East L.A.

Toward the end of the journal, Nicholas Tyson wrote:

I watched the film today, and I was literally sickened. Filth. Alex and Rich saw it, too. Alex broke down and cried. I watched it a second time with them. There's no way the police are going to go after B.S. Someone inside the Hollywood PD, and more than likely the D.A.'s office, is on his payroll. We've decided to continue gathering evidence on our own and complete the book. In the interim, we can only pray more young women don't fall victim to his secret hunger for violence.

"My God."

Sara's voice snapped him back to the present. He glanced at her, saw terrible knowledge in his eyes. He felt that same awful knowing in his own heart.

"I'll bet the farm that B.S. is Blaine Stocker," Nick said.

"We need to find out who he is."

Sara rose on legs that weren't quite steady and paced to the kitchen window. Outside, the rain had stopped, but a thick fog had rolled in from the cape.

Absently, she touched the burgeoning bruise on her forehead. "I think your father and my parents were working on a book."

"Or a documentary."

She turned to him. "Is there a possibility

the manuscript could be packed away with your father's belongings? Maybe at your mother's house?"

"Mom went through all of my father's things when he was killed. She was angry. Most of it went to charity. The rest went into the trash."

"Is there any way you can get into her house and check?"

"I've got a key," he said. "Maybe I can duck in while my mother's at the shop."

"Thank you."

He joined her at the window, his expression troubled. Beyond the glass, fog swirled around the juniper and rock. "In the interim, you can't stay here alone."

"Maybe there's a motel off the highway."

He remained silent for so long that for a moment, Sara thought he wouldn't respond. Finally, he turned to her, his eyes seeking hers, holding them with such intensity that she needed to look away, but couldn't. "Your things are already at my bungalow. Stay with me. You'll be safe. We can work on this thing together."

It was the logical thing to do. Practical.

But, a refusal teetered on her lips. Maybe because of the way he was looking at her. As if she were the only woman in the world and he was the loneliest man on earth.

"All right," she said.

Something she didn't understand flashed in his eyes. "Bring everything you've found so far," he said. "Notes. Photos. The journal. Anything you can think of."

"What are we going to do?"

"I'm going to get into some dry clothes. Then we're going to sit down and figure this thing out, starting with the name Blaine Stocker."

NICK HAD ALWAYS prided himself on his level-headedness. His ability to keep his cool under pressure. On taking the high road over the low. On doing the right thing even when the right thing wasn't necessarily the easiest.

Until tonight, anyway.

Inviting Sara to stay with him was a train wreck waiting to happen. He was too attracted to her. Too willing to let down his guard. And far too willing to set aside his reservations for the promise of a touch or the taste of her lips. A hell of a dilemma for a man who'd sworn he was going to be smart about this and steadfast in his convictions.

The fog thickened on the drive from the mansion to his bungalow. Visibility dwindled to less than twenty feet. As his cruiser crept along at a snail's pace, he knew neither of them would be going anywhere the rest of the night.

Inside, Nick locked all the doors, then headed for the second bedroom, which he'd turned into a sort of home office. He picked up his laptop and carried it to the kitchen table and turned it on.

"Nick, you should put on some dry clothes."

He glanced at her as the laptop booted. "In a minute."

"What are you doing?"

"Checking on the status of my inquiry with the Missing and Unidentified Persons Unit." Taking a chair, he sat. "And seeing what we can find on Blaine Stocker."

His hands danced across the keyboard as he brought up the Department of Justice database. "Here it is," he said, leaning forward.

Sara bent and read the report. "Jenna

Sherwood. Twenty-four years old. Reported missing. Status: unresolved."

"She was reported missing and never found," Nick said.

Sara didn't know anything about the young woman, but the fact that she'd never been found saddened her. "Do you think she's dead?"

"No way to tell at this point. I'll forward the stills and see if the techies at the Unit can match them." Nick logged out of the database, then pulled up a search engine and typed in the name Blaine Stocker.

The inquiry returned several dozen hits. "Popular guy," he muttered and clicked on the first link.

Sara leaned over his shoulder as he read the headline from the *Los Angeles Times* newspaper dated just over a year ago.

Former Hollywood Director Suffers Massive Stroke.
In his heyday, Blaine Stocker was one of the hottest and most controversial moviemakers in the business. The director of over a dozen films, including

The Dread and *Come Hither the Night*, Stocker's talents invariably leaned toward the dark and artistic side of film-making. After suffering a minor stroke two years ago, however, he retired to his home in San Francisco with his wife, Channing, and virtually disappeared from the Hollywood scene. Rumor had it he was working on another movie when a second stroke rendered him unable to work just six weeks ago....

"A Hollywood director?" Taking the chair next to him, Sara shot Nick a puzzled look. "I don't get it. How does he tie in to all of this?"

"Maybe there's a Hollywood connection," Nick answered.

Her eyes widened. "My God. Snuff?"

"Could be."

"And my parents? Your father? How do they tie in?"

"Your parents were Hollywood insiders."

"Maybe it's like we said. A book. Your father and my parents were trying to expose him."

"Some proof would be nice."

She nibbled on a nail, her eyes never leaving

the laptop screen. "If this Stocker dude suffered a stroke, he's probably feeble. There's no way he stole those notes or pushed me today."

"Yeah, but he's got enough money to pay people to do his dirty work for him." Nick clicked on the second link. The story focused on the former director's slow recovery from a series of strokes that had left him partially paralyzed.

One by one, they went through each link. Sara jotted notes while Nick maneuvered the mouse. It took almost an hour to get through all the links. Afterward, Nick knew a lot more about Blaine Stocker. But he had no idea how any of it tied in to what happened twenty years ago.

"Any word from the lab?" Sara asked.

Nick shook his head. "Might take a couple of days."

"There's no link between Stocker and my parents," Sara said.

Hearing the frustration in her voice, Nick glanced over at her. "San Francisco isn't that far."

Her eyes widened, her hand already

reaching for the laptop. "I'll make myself a reservation tonight—"

Nick set his hand over hers. "If you go, I go with you."

That silenced her, but only for a moment. "You'd do that?"

He knew accompanying her to San Francisco would probably be a mistake. She was already messing with his head, making him want her. Making him want things that would only complicate his life. But looking into her eyes, he thought he'd probably jump through a flaming hoop just to see her smile.

"There's a commuter flight that leaves the Shelter Cove Airport first thing in the morning," he heard himself say. "The return is late, so it would only be a day trip."

"We won't need much time." She glanced at her watch. "Maybe I should see if I can find Blaine Stocker's phone number, give him a call and set up an appointment."

Nick shook his head. "This might be one of those times when it's better to surprise him. Catch him off guard."

Looking restless, she tapped her fingers

against the table. "So what do we do in the interim?"

He glanced at his wet clothes. "I think the first order of the day is some dry clothes."

"I'm sorry." Her glaze flicked over him. "You've been sitting here all this time in damp clothes."

He waved off the statement, but her concern warmed him in a way it shouldn't have. Not at all comfortable with that, he motioned toward the notes and papers they'd brought with them from the house. "Maybe we could go through what you've found so far and see if we can come up with a connection or some angle we haven't seen yet."

She was already reaching for the folder containing the pages she'd printed at the library when he started for the shower.

Ten minutes later he found Sara sitting at his dining room table, every scrap of information on the deaths of their parents spread out before her. On the stove, a saucepan steamed, and he realized she'd heated soup.

"I hope you like chicken noodle."

"Grew up on it." But Nick wasn't thinking about soup. He couldn't take his eyes off

Sara—the way she looked, sitting at his table, her attention fastened to the papers in front of her. Even pale, a bruise the size of a walnut forming on her forehead, she was one of the most beautiful women he'd ever laid eyes on. She was determined and smart and brave and he suddenly had the urge to go to her and take her mouth in a kiss. He knew better than to entertain inappropriate thoughts at a time when he needed to keep his distance. But she didn't exactly invoke his best judgment.

"I'll make an ice pack for that bruise," he said.

"It doesn't hurt." She gave him only half of her attention as she paged through a mountain of papers.

"If you don't get that swelling down, you'll feel it in the morning." He carried bowls to the table and set one in front of her. "Sorry for canned food. The scourge of a bachelor."

She glanced up from the paper she was reading. An emotion he didn't understand scrolled across her features, then her expression turned somber. "Sonia told me about your late wife, Nick. I've been so caught up in this, I didn't broach the subject. But I wanted you to know I'm sorry."

The statement shouldn't have taken him by surprise, but even after a year he invariably had a difficult time knowing how to respond. He didn't like condolences. Didn't like remembering those dark months following Nancy's death.

She must have noticed his reaction because she set the paper down and set her hand over his. "I shouldn't have brought it up. I'm such a klutz."

"You're not."

"You okay?"

"Sure."

Judging from the way she was looking at him, he figured it was a safe bet they both knew he wasn't. Not that he wanted to talk about it. He didn't. Not now. Not ever. That was how he'd dealt with the loss. The pain. In the year since the accident, Nick hadn't discussed Nancy's death with anyone. He hadn't told a soul she'd been eight weeks pregnant. Or that for months afterward he'd struggled with nightmares and flashbacks and cold sweats in the middle of the night.

Shoving the dark memories aside, Nick began to pace. An uncomfortable restlessness stirred inside him, as if he didn't quite fit into his own skin.

"You're going to wear a path in the tile."

He turned to look at her, knowing immediately his expression was too intense, too serious. Too…sad.

"That was a joke." She gave him a tentative smile.

He hoped his smile looked real. "Not my strong point."

An uncomfortable silence ensued. Sara glanced down at the papers in front of her. After a moment, Nick took the chair next to her. He wasn't close, but near enough to get a whiff of her perfume. The scent went to his head like a powerful narcotic, making him a little dizzy.

"Okay," he began. "Let's take a look at everything you've got and see if we can make sense of it."

Sara glanced down at her notes. "We have the reel-to-reel."

"The newspaper stories, one of which puts my father and your mother together at a café."

"With an unidentified manuscript," Sara added. "That has yet to be found."

"The notes that were stolen from you."

"An anonymous caller."

"And an unidentified perp who nearly pushed you off that cliff and left two threatening messages."

Her gaze met his. Within the depth of her gypsy eyes Nick saw fear. But it was tempered with a firm resolve to do what she needed to do to solve a mystery that became more complex and grew uglier with each layer they peeled away.

"They were working on a book," she said.

"A true-crime book that would have ruined Blaine Stocker."

"He was killing women," she said in that same hollow voice. "Filming it."

"Selling it to the highest bidder as snuff."

"That's incredibly…evil," she said.

But Nick's mind was already jumping ahead with some very ugly scenarios. Not only of young women being killed, but of a young crime writer and a prominent Hollywood couple who might have been murdered for the knowledge they possessed. Knowledge they'd planned to expose in a very public way.

"This is almost too wild to believe," Sara said.

"Stocker wouldn't have wanted information like this becoming public," he said carefully.

He knew it the instant his meaning registered. Her eyes widened. What little color was left in her cheeks drained. "You think Blaine Stocker is responsible for their deaths?"

"Think about it. Your parents and my father were about to ruin him in a very big way."

"So he murdered them, and made it look like murder-suicide."

"We can't be certain, but it's an angle definitely worth looking into." He hit a key on the laptop and shoved it at her. "Have you ever seen him before?"

Sara looked at the photo of a young Blaine Stocker. He was in some upscale Hollywood restaurant with a laughing blonde on his arm. Sara stared at the photo as if transfixed.

"What is it?" Nick pressed. "Do you recognize him? Was he there that night?"

"I don't know. Maybe. He seems familiar, but I don't know where I've seen him. I don't even know if I've ever met him." Lowering her head slightly, she rubbed at both temples with her fingertips. "Damn it."

The urge to go to her, set his hands on her shoulders and massage away the aches was strong, but Nick didn't move.

"Headache?" he asked.

"Not from the bump." She glanced at him over her fingertips and offered a wan smile. "Frustration."

He offered a smile. "Sooner or later this will come together."

"I'm not so sure." Her expression turned thoughtful. "If Stocker is responsible for the deaths of our parents, who's the anonymous caller and what's his motivation?"

Nick considered the question a moment and shook his head. "If Stocker was involved in the making of snuff films, maybe someone who knows about it wants him to pay."

"But that doesn't make any sense. Why involve me?"

"I don't know." But a chill formed at the base of his spine. "Maybe someone is using you to find something. Someone else is willing to kill to keep that from happening."

He didn't miss the quiver that ran the length of her. "Do you think the man who assaulted me and the anonymous caller are two different people?" she asked.

"Possibly. Two people. Two different agendas. That's what we have to figure out."

Her gaze met his. He didn't like the pale cast to her complexion or the way her hands shook slightly when she set them in front of her. "It's been twenty years. I can't help but wonder what the catalyst is."

"Maybe that's one of the questions Blaine Stocker can answer tomorrow."

Chapter Eleven

By ten o'clock the next morning, Nick and Sara had arrived in San Francisco, rented a car and were heading north on Hwy 101 toward the exclusive Sea Cliff neighborhood where Blaine Stocker and his wife lived.

Having resided in California her entire life, Sara had seen some lovely homes. But when they turned onto 25th Avenue and the Stocker estate loomed into view, the stunning beauty of it took her breath away.

Lush sago palms, eight-foot-high stucco walls and scrolled iron gates shrouded the sprawling Mediterranean-style mansion. As Nick stopped at the security gate, Sara could see past the mansion to the deep-blue water of the bay and, beyond, the span of the Golden Gate Bridge.

"What do we tell security?" she asked, worried by the possibility that they'd traveled this far only to be turned away.

"I'll think of something," Nick said and hit the intercom button.

A tinny voice came over the line. "May I help you?"

"This is Officer Nick Tyson with the Cape Darkwood PD. I'm here to see Blaine Stocker."

"I don't see your name on the appointment list."

"I'm not on the list." Nick paused. "You a cop?"

"Former," the voice said, with a little too much pride.

"SFPD?"

"Mark Lewinski. LAPD. Sixteen years."

"In that case, Mr. Lewinski, I suggest you check my credentials, pronto, unless you want me to come back with a warrant and an army of officers who will be happy to tear this place apart and cart your ass off to the station for a few hours." He lowered his voice. "Just between you and me, I'd rather do this the easy way."

Silence reigned for perhaps a full minute,

then Lewinski said. "I'll call your department and get right back to you."

"Fair enough."

Leaning back, he set his hands on the wheel and gave her a smile.

"Effective," she said.

"It's that cop brotherhood thing. Works every time."

Still, Sara couldn't help but worry. Even if they got in, would Stocker speak to them?

The gate jolted and groaned open. "Drive around and park beneath the portico at the front of the house," came the tinny voice.

"Roger that," Nick said and drove through the gate.

The house was set into a hill and surrounded with verdant trees. The creamy stucco contrasted nicely with the barrel-tile roof. It was one of the most spectacular homes Sara had ever seen.

Nick parked and shut down the engine. A middle-aged man in a charcoal suit approached from the front door, ducked slightly to make eye contact with both of them, then opened Nick's door.

"Welcome to the Stocker estate." It was

the man from the intercom. "I'm Lewinski, head of security."

Nick slid from the car. "Thanks for making this easy for all of us."

"What's this about?"

"I'd rather discuss that with Mr. Stocker first."

Lewinski sneered.

Sara got out of the car and met the two men as they stood near the driver's-side door. Lewinski frowned at her when she approached.

"This way." He led them down a flagstone path toward the side of the mansion where a fountain spewed water high into the air and oleander bloomed in profusion. At a side door, Lewinski turned to Nick. "Raise your arms. Gotta pat you down."

Nick arched a brow, but did as he was told. "Does Mr. Stocker subject all his visitors to a frisk?"

"Just the ones he doesn't know."

The man turned to Sara. Her heart began to pound. She didn't want to blow this, but she didn't want him to touch her.

"Take off your jacket and give him your bag," Nick said to her as if reading her mind.

He took her purse and handed it to Lewinski. "She's clean," he said.

Frowning, Lewinski rummaged through the bag, even digging into the zipper pockets on the inside.

When he was finished, Sara held up her jacket. "I'm not armed," she said.

Scowling, Lewinski took the jacket and quickly searched the pockets. Evidently convinced the pair were unarmed, he opened the beveled-glass door and ushered them inside.

"This way."

He led them through a wide foyer adorned with fresh-cut flowers, a chandelier the size of a small car and marble-tiled floors as shiny as wet glass. From there they proceeded down a narrow hall with tall ceilings and arched doorways. Every inch of wall space was covered with framed photos of Hollywood celebrities. Sara took in a black-and-white shot of a handsome man in a white tux embracing a youthful Marilyn Monroe. James Garner in a cowboy hat and boots astride a beautiful spotted horse. Sara recognized Sharon Tate. Liza Minelli. There were dozens of other Hollywood big shots she didn't recognize.

Then they were standing in a huge room paneled in dark wood. Two walls were comprised of books. A hearth dominated the third wall. The west wall was constructed totally of mullioned-glass windows and a series of paneled French doors that opened to a patio that offered a stunning view of the bay and the Golden Gate Bridge.

A woman in a designer suit with tastefully coiffed silver hair stood at the window like some elegant sentinel. Sara guessed her to be well into her seventies, but she had a powerful presence. Dark, all-seeing eyes swept from Nick to Sara and then back to Nick.

"Who are you and what do you want?" she asked in a deep and cultured voice.

Nick stepped forward and extended his hand. "I'm Nick Tyson, Chief of Police up in Cape Darkwood."

An emotion Sara didn't quite recognize flashed in the woman's eyes as she accepted his hand. "Are you any relation to Nicholas Tyson, the true-crime writer?"

"He was my father."

"You look very much like him." A smile

overtook her face, then she turned her attention to Sara. "And you?"

"I'm Sara Douglas." She shook the woman's hand, taking in the firm grip and cool, thin skin.

"My God, you're the picture of Alex."

"You knew my parents?"

"Everyone knows everyone in Hollywood, darling." The woman lifted an elegant shoulder. "We ran in the same circles."

"You must be Channing Stocker," Nick ventured.

She gave them a regal smile. "May I ask what brings you all the way from Cape Darkwood?"

"We'd like to ask Mr. Stocker some questions," Sara said.

The woman's attention snapped to Sara. "What kind of questions?"

"About something that happened twenty years ago," Nick put in.

Channing's eyes narrowed. "Are you talking about the murder-suicide at the Douglas mansion?"

"Is Mr. Stocker available?" Nick asked.

The woman studied them for so long that

Sara thought she wouldn't answer. Then she turned with the grace of a dramatic actor and swept to the French doors and pulled them open. "I'm not sure how much help he'll be. You see, he had a second stroke last month."

Sara stared at the frail old man sitting in the wheelchair. His spine curved so that his chin was nearly to his chest. A thin line of drool dribbled onto his silk smoking jacket. With the poise of a highly paid model, Channing strode to his chair, bent to blot the saliva, then positioned herself behind the chair and pushed him into the room.

"He likes to sit in the sunshine and fresh air in the morning," she said cheerfully. "The doctors say it's good for him, so we sit out here as much as possible." A small smile lit her mouth when she contemplated Sara and Nick. "Would either of you like a drink? Bloody Mary? Tequila Sunrise?"

"It's a little early for me, ma'am," Nick said.

Sara couldn't take her eyes off the shrunken old man. Until this moment, Blaine Stocker had been a vague threat. Possibly guilty of unspeakable crimes.

The man in the wheelchair wasn't capable

of any of those things. His body was frail and shrunken and bent. The left side of his face drooped slightly. An oxygen tube ran along both cheeks to his nose. But his eyes were the eyes of a much younger man. They burned with intelligence and a cunning that made gooseflesh rise on Sara's arms. It was as if he were trapped within a body that had failed him.

"Mr. Stocker, we'd like to ask you a few questions, if that's all right," Sara said.

His eyes landed on her. She nearly winced at the power of his stare. Recognition quivered inside her. She stared, knowing she'd met him at some point in her life, but unable to remember where or when.

An arthritic finger moved and the motorized wheelchair drew closer. The old man gave a minute nod. It was still early in the day, yet Channing walked to the wet bar and poured orange juice and tequila into tall glass tumblers.

"You can use those chairs if you like," she said, motioning toward two wingback chairs sitting opposite a large mahogany desk.

Nick dragged them to the wheelchair. Sara

seated herself and Nick took the other so that they were both facing Blaine Stocker.

"We were wondering if you could help us sort through some information," Nick began.

The old man's eyes shifted to Nick. "What…information?" His voice was as rough as a saw chewing through wood. The left side of his mouth didn't move when he spoke.

"You were a director." Smoothly Nick handed him a card. "I've enjoyed your films over the years. The *Falcon at Midnight* was my favorite."

"I liked *The Dread*," Sara put in.

The old man's hand shook as he accepted the card, but his eyes lit up as if someone had flipped a switch. Within the depths of his gaze, Sara saw an odd mix of pride and ego. Because it was apparently difficult for him to speak, he nodded.

Nick continued. "But there were other films, too, weren't there, Mr. Stocker?"

"What…films?"

Nick removed several stills he'd had made from the snuff film they'd recovered at the mansion. "A…documentary, perhaps."

The old man's gaze swept to the stills. His eyes widened. His mouth opened. His lips quivered. His frail body jolted.

"We know about the women," Nick said.

The old man began to shake. "No."

Nick displayed the second still. A black-and-white depicting a terrible scene. "You made other films, too, didn't you, Mr. Stocker?"

"Not me…"

"We have the film. The proof. We also have the notes."

The old man's eyes rolled back white. "No…"

Setting her drink on the desk, Mrs. Stocker strode quickly over. "How dare you come into my home and insult my husband?"

"These are his," Nick said.

Channing Stocker bent to look at the stills. All color bled from her face, but her eyes remained strong. She leveled those eyes on Nick. "I don't know why you're here or what you think you know, but I want you to leave."

Sara reached out to touch her. "Please, Mrs. Stocker, we think your husband may know something about these murders."

Angrily, the woman shook off her hand. "Get out. Both of you. Now."

Nick thrust one of the stills at the old man. "Did you murder this woman?" Anger resonated in his voice. "Did you film it?"

"If you don't leave, I'm going to call the police."

Sara sat in the chair, her heart pounding, unable to take her eyes off the frail elderly man before them. She hadn't expected Nick to go after him so hard.

Nick ignored the woman and focused on Stocker. "Talk to us," he said. "I'll make sure the police know you cooperated."

"What the hell is going on here?"

The deep male voice boomed like a gunshot. Nick stood abruptly and faced the door. Sara did the same to see a exquisitely dressed man of about thirty-five years stride toward them. Eyes as black and cunning as the old man's swept from Sara to Nick. "Who are you people and what are you doing here?"

When neither of them answered, his eyes went to Mrs. Stocker. "Mother, what's going on here?"

"He claims to be a police officer with questions about the Douglas-Tyson murders up in Cape Darkwood." Channing Stocker's hand shook when she brought the glass to her lips. "Lewinski checked him out. I thought Blaine might be able to help them."

The man's eyes landed on Nick. "Let me see your ID."

Nick reached for his wallet and flashed his badge. "I'm with the Cape Darkwood PD," he said. "And who are you?"

"I'm Brett Stocker." He motioned toward the old man in the wheelchair. "Blaine is my father. And you are trespassing."

Nick shoved his wallet back into his pocket. "We have reason to believe your father may be able to help us solve the murders of several women."

"Murder?" Brett Stocker choked out a laugh. "Are you insane?" He motioned toward his father. "Look at him! Does he look like a dangerous man to you?"

"Mr. Stocker," Sara began, "these murders happened a long time ago."

Stocker glared at her. "We are not inclined to answer any more questions."

"If you don't cooperate, I'll have no choice but to take what proof I have to the FBI." Nick shrugged. "I thought you might want to protect your old man from that kind of publicity."

Brett's eyes went from Nick to his mother, to his father. "Look, I don't know what you people are up to, but my father is a good man. There's no way he's involved in anything illegal, especially murder. He's a philanthropist with an impeccable reputation. How dare you walk into his home and attack his character."

The elder Stocker raised his head, his eyes flicking to Nick. "Get…out."

Brett walked over to this father and squeezed his thin shoulder. "It's okay, Dad. I'll handle this."

"We're just trying to find out what happened," Sara said. "We thought he might be able to help us."

"If you people had some kind of evidence, the cops would be all over this." He shook his head. "You don't have anything. You're fishing. Probably trying to generate some negative publicity." He snarled. "Parasites."

Nick flashed the final still at the elder Stocker. "We know what you did, old man. We'll be back when we have proof."

Channing Stocker strode to her husband's side. "This interview is over. If you don't leave now, I'll call the police and have you arrested for trespassing."

Sara had never seen Nick like this. Angry and pushing boundaries. She moved toward the door, hoping he would follow.

But Nick held his ground, his eyes never leaving Blaine Stocker. "We're not finished with this."

Crossing to Nick, Brett slapped the photo from his hand. "Get out and take your worthless accusations with you."

Certain Nick was going to launch himself at the man, Sara strode quickly forward and took his arm. "Let's go."

Nick didn't budge.

Brett Stocker's lip curled. "Mother, call 911."

In her peripheral vision, Sara was aware of the woman setting down her drink, walking to the desk and picking up the phone.

"Nick," she said. "Let's go."

Nick resisted a moment longer, then turned and started for the door.

Lewinski appeared at the doorway. His jacket stood open. At his side, Sara saw a leather holster and the blue steel of a pistol. "You heard the man," he said. "Out. Now."

Nick glared at Brett Stocker. "If I were you, I'd get your old man a good lawyer. He won't do well in prison, believe me."

Lunging forward, Lewinski shoved Nick toward the door. "Unless you and your lady friend want to spend the night in jail, I suggest you move your ass. *Now!*"

For a terrible moment, Sara thought Nick was going to punch the guy. Hoping to avoid a fight—and possible arrest—she once again started toward the door. Behind her, she heard Nick follow, Lewinski bringing up the rear. "Sorry about this, Mr. Stocker," he said.

"Get them out of here," Brett snarled. "I'll deal with you later."

Sara barely noticed the opulence of the mansion as she moved down the hall toward the door from which they'd entered. She could hear Nick and Lewinski behind her. She sensed the gun in the latter man's hand, wondered if he had it pointed at Nick's back. Or hers.

Outside, in the sunshine and crisp breeze off the bay, she felt dirty, felt the sudden need to wash her hands. Nick made eye contact with her as they headed toward the rental car.

"That was productive as hell," he muttered sarcastically.

"I recognized the old man," she said.

He shot her a questioning look. "From where?"

"I don't know, but I've definitely seen him before."

Nick glanced over his shoulder as he yanked open the car door and slid inside. Lewinski stood on the porch, his eyes hidden behind dark shades, the pistol in his hand.

Nick put the car in gear. "That son of a bitch knows something," he said.

As they pulled out of the driveway and onto the street of the exclusive neighborhood, all Sara could wonder was what.

Chapter Twelve

Full darkness had fallen by the time Nick and Sara reached his bungalow. Sara hated it that the trip to San Francisco had been a wash. Only now did she realize she'd been overly optimistic in hoping Blaine Stocker would give up his secrets easily. He might be old and frail, but she'd seen the remnants of the young man he'd once been in his eyes. A young man who'd evidently had a dark side.

The lingering aroma of that morning's coffee welcomed them when they entered the bungalow. "I've got steaks in the freezer," Nick said, tossing his keys onto the counter.

They hadn't eaten since noon, but Sara wasn't hungry. She was still keyed up, her mind replaying everything that had happened.

As if knowing how she felt, Nick gave her

a half smile. "I've also got a nice bottle of merlot that's been sitting around gathering dust."

"Good place to start," she said.

He walked to the bar, pulled out a bottle and proceeded to uncork it. Sara found a couple of stemmed glasses in the cabinet and carried them to the bar. "Sorry I lost my temper earlier," he said.

"You're entitled."

He poured, then raised his glass. "Here's to uncovering secrets."

"And vindicating my father." She clinked her glass to his.

Gazes holding, they sipped. "It's good," she said.

"Local vineyard. French grapes."

"I didn't know you were a connoisseur of wine."

"I'm not, but my dad was. He tried to teach me, but I was too young to fully appreciate it."

"I didn't realize until today how hard this must be for you, too," she said.

"It's okay. I was skeptical, but that old man recognized those photos." The muscles in his jaws went taut. "I think that son of bitch killed them."

"Me, too."

Shaking his head, Nick set his glass on the counter and walked to the living room. Sara watched from the bar as he went to the hearth for wood and kindling and built a fire.

She joined him a few minutes later and sat down beside him. "All these years and it still hurts."

"It was bad enough losing them the way we did. But for the killer to frame your father... For him to portray your mother and my father as adulterers..." As if at a loss, he let the words trail.

"The person responsible destroyed our families," Sara said.

Nick stared into the flames. "Because they were going to expose him for what he was."

"The maker of snuff films."

"It's a logical assumption."

"What do we do now? It seems like we've reached a dead end."

His gaze met hers. Hard-edged determination churned within their depths, and Sara knew now that he believed her he wouldn't give up until Stocker was behind bars. "We have one more source of information we haven't tapped into."

Her mind spun through the players. Blaine Stocker. Channing Stocker. Nick's mother, Laurel. Her own fractured memory. "Who?"

"The lead detective who investigated the case."

"Of course." Excitement jumped through her at the thought. "Henry James."

"He retired ten years ago. You remember him?"

"He was kind to me. I always liked him. I didn't realize it at the time, but I think he always believed I saw the killer that night."

"What makes you think that?"

"He questioned me quite a bit about it. He was the one who recommended hypnosis." Remembering the countless sessions with several psychologists and therapists, she shook her head. "Nothing ever panned out. I could see the man, but I couldn't recall his face, and I could never identify him."

"Pretty horrific scene for a seven-year-old kid."

Even now the memory of that night made

her shudder. "It was bad, Nick. Ugly. To see your parents like that. The blood. Knowing they were gone forever. It's like your worst nightmare becoming reality."

For a moment she thought he would put his arm around her or perhaps set his hand over hers. But he continued to stare into the fire. She wasn't sure if she was glad for it…or disappointed.

"Let me see if I can find a current number or address for Detective James." Rising, he walked to the bar and opened his laptop.

Sara remained at the hearth and sipped her wine, but it had gone sour on her tongue. Had they reached a dead end? Or would the retired detective be able to help them?

At the bar, Nick tapped keys. The computer beeped and he sighed. "He retired a few months after the case closed and moved to Phoenix. I've got a phone number."

She glanced at her watch. "It's not yet nine o'clock…"

"Let's call him and see what he has to say." Nick picked up the cordless phone and punched in numbers. Sara held her breath, hoping the detective would be able to help them put the final pieces of the puzzle together.

"Henry James, please."

Nick's voice drew her from her dark thoughts. She watched his face. "How did it happen?" he asked.

Sara saw his jaw tighten, his brows knit. "I'm sorry to have bothered you, ma'am." He hung up the phone and shook his head.

She could tell by the look in his eyes that the news was not good. "What?"

"He passed away in a motor vehicle mishap a few months after retiring," he said.

"Oh no!" Even though the prospect of gaining helpful information from the former detective had been a long shot, Sara felt the words like a gut punch. "A car accident?"

"Hit and run." His expression hardened. "Someone ran him off the highway."

"Did the police find the person responsible?"

"No."

Suspicion spun through Sara's mind like shards of glass, cutting through the last remnants of hope. A dozen scenarios rose inside her. One look at Nick and she knew he was thinking the same thing. "Do you think he was murdered?"

"I think it's a possibility."

Needing to move, Sara rose and began to pace, her wine forgotten. "My God, Nick, if it wasn't an accident…" Her words trailed; she could barely bring herself to utter them. "Someone killed him to cover their tracks."

"Keep him from digging," Nick added.

The thought sent a shudder through her that went all the way to her bones. "How are we going to prove any of this?"

"We keep digging until we find something concrete." He tossed her a sage look. "Until we blow this thing open, I don't want you out of my sight."

An argument drifted through her mind, but Sara didn't voice it. She didn't want to admit it, but she was scared. If Stocker could kill a trained detective, he could get to anyone.…

"All right," she replied.

"No one knows you're here with me," Nick said. "Let's keep it that way."

"Okay. I can do that." She looked at him. "But I'm not going to sit around and do nothing."

He approached her, his eyes going hard. "You can't go back to the mansion. I've got two officers working for me. The Cape Darkwood budget can't afford for me to pay one of them to babysit you."

"I wouldn't ask you to do that."

A quiver went through her when he set his hands on her shoulders. "Someone is trying to kill you," he said. "They almost succeeded yesterday. I'm not going to give them another chance."

She didn't want to make eye contact. There were too many emotions inside her, too close to the surface. She knew that once she looked into his eyes she would be lost.

"Look at me, damn it."

The pull to him was too powerful; she wasn't strong enough to resist. Like a swimmer caught in a current, she would be swept away and drowned. She only continued stare at the floor, he cupped her chin and turned her face to him.

She felt the contact like an electric current running the length of her body. Heat and shock and a dozen other sensations she couldn't begin to name.

"Why are you shaking?" he whispered.

"Because there are other things going on that scare me, too."

"You mean between us?" His gaze searched hers.

"Yes."

"It scares me, too."

"What are we going to do about it?"

"Take it slow," he said. "Like this."

The floor caved in beneath her feet when he lowered his mouth to hers. The electrical pulses she'd felt earlier shot outward and exploded in every nerve ending. Her body went rigid. With shock. With pleasure. With the intellectual knowledge this was going to complicate an already complicated situation.

But for the first time in her life, Sara didn't care about logic. She didn't care about doing the right thing. Or playing it safe.

Banking the little voice telling her to stop, she kissed him back with an abandon that shocked and thrilled. Slow and easy turned fast and ravenous. His mouth moved over hers as if he wanted to devour her. Sara felt that same hunger rising inside her. The urgent need to feel his hands on her body.

The equally powerful need to touch him and explore every hard male inch of him.

He kissed her until she was dizzy with pleasure. Drunk on the electric hum of desire. Until bells clanged in her ears and her heart thrummed like thunder.

"The door," he growled as his mouth moved over hers.

Only then did she realize the sound of bells ringing in her ears was the doorbell. "Might be important."

The bell rang again. Groaning, Nick pulled away. He glanced down at himself, and Sara realized he couldn't answer the door without revealing more than either of them wanted revealed.

Grumbling beneath his breath, he grabbed a windbreaker off a coat rack, tied it around his waist and checked the peephole. Sara saw him pause, draw a breath, then open the door.

"Mom," he said.

Laurel Tyson walked into the living room without waiting for an invitation. Her eyes swept the room, her expression going cold and hard when she spotted Sara. Her smile fell. She stood as rigid as an ice sculpture, her eyes moving to her son.

"I didn't know you had company," she said.

"Had you called before dropping in," Nick replied levelly, "I would have told you."

"What is she doing here?" As if realizing the question was superfluous, Laurel raised her hands. "Never mind. I think it's obvious."

Nick stared at his mother, his expression stony. "Is there something I can do for you, Mom?"

"I can't believe you let her get to you."

"You're out of line," he said.

"And you're just like your father," she snarled.

Realizing the situation was about to spiral out of control, Sara stepped forward. "Mrs. Tyson, don't be angry. Please. We have something to tell you."

Laurel's attention snapped to Sara. "I have no interest in hearing anything you have to say."

Undaunted, Sara continued. "Nick and I have been looking into what happened twenty years ago."

"I'll bet."

"We believe things didn't happen the way the police said they did."

"Or maybe my son is drawn to you the same way my husband was drawn to your mother."

Sara nearly winced at the loathing that seethed in the woman's eyes. "Your husband and my mother were not involved. And my father didn't kill anyone."

"How dare you dredge up all that pain in a desperate attempt to clear your father's name?"

"There was someone else in that room," Sara shot back. "A man with a gun. He shot them because they were working on a tell-all book. A book that would have ruined a wealthy Hollywood director and sent him to prison."

"That's absurd. A wild story fabricated because you can't deal with the truth."

Nick turned to his mother. "It's true. We think Blaine Stocker was involved in the making of snuff films. Dad was collaborating on a book with Richard and Alexandra Douglas. Stocker went after them, murdered them, planted evidence to make it look like a murder-suicide. The local media was all too happy to accommodate him."

He motioned toward Sara. "Yesterday, someone tried to push her off the cliffs behind the house. They almost succeeded."

The older woman's gaze went to Sara, but there was no concern, no sympathy in their depths. "I don't believe you." Her eyes went to Nick. "Either of you." Her gaze flicked to the jacket tied around his waist and she shook her head. "Nick, I thought you were too smart to fall for a pretty face. Then again your father evidently had the same weakness, didn't he?"

"That's enough," Nick snapped.

Knowing the scene was only going to get worse, Sara intervened. "We have your husband's research notes. We also have an eight-millimeter film we believe was made by Blaine Stocker."

"But what you really want is those claws of yours in my son, don't you?" Eyes narrowing, her body gathering as if to pounce, she approached Sara. "Your mother was my closest friend. I loved her like a sister. I trusted her. She betrayed me by sleeping with my husband. It disgusts me that her daughter is doing the same with my son."

"That's enough." Nick stepped between the two women, but his eyes were on his mother. "You need to put your bitterness aside and listen."

She glared at her son. "Alex blinded Nicholas with her neediness. With her sexual charms. With that phony decency people saw when they looked at her." Her gaze went to Sara and she shook her head. "And now her daughter is blinding you."

"That's not true," Sara defended. "All we want is to expose the truth."

"You want a hell of a lot more than that, you little slut." She made a sound of disgust. "Evidently, my son is more than happy to give it to you."

The words struck her with the same shock and violence as the slap Laurel had delivered two days before. Emotions tightened Sara's throat until she thought she would choke. But she held back the tears. Bit back the anger. Deflected the pain.

Vaguely, she was aware of Nick standing a few feet away, shaking his head. Laurel reached the door, yanked it open. The sound of rain entered the bungalow, but Sara's attention was focused on the woman staring at her as if she wanted to do bodily harm.

"He'll never love you, Sara. He'll let you use him. He'll use you, too. But he'll never love you the way he loved Nancy and the baby."

The door slammed hard enough to rattle the windows. Even though Laurel had left, the tension remained. Sara's mind reeled with all the hateful things that had been said. She could feel herself shaking, both inside and out. All the while Laurel's parting words echoed inside her head like some terrible mantra.

He'll never love you the way he loved Nancy and the baby.

Baby? What baby?

Sara didn't want to look at Nick. She was afraid if she did the question would be plastered all over her face. Or that the dam would break and once it did she wouldn't be able to stop it.

"I'm sorry about that," he said after a moment.

She didn't look at him. "She's wrong about my mother."

"She's wrong about a lot of things."

"Why does she hate me so much?" When her voice cracked, she turned away and strode to the sink, fighting tears. "Damn it."

She jolted when he came up behind her and set his hands on her shoulders. "Because she's bitter. Because you remind her of your mother."

"My mother didn't betray her."

"I know." Gently, he turned her to face him. When she wouldn't look at him, he put his fingers beneath her chin and raised her face. "I'm not going to make excuses for my mother. But she lost a lot that night. I think maybe she lost more than she could bear."

"All of us lost more than we could bear."

"We're going to get through this. We're going to find the truth. And we're going to make sure the person responsible pays."

For the first time, Sara looked into his eyes. Within their depths she saw all the things she so desperately needed to see. Understanding. Compassion. The determination to find the truth no matter what obstacles were thrown in his path.

"Thank you for saying that."

Dipping his head slightly, he gave her a small smile. "Don't cry."

"I'm not." It was a silly thing to say; she was definitely crying. "Damn it."

"You are."

She choked out a sound that was part sob, part laugh and wiped her cheeks with the back of her hand. "For twenty years I've been told my father was a murderer. I've been told my mother was unfaithful to him. There were times when I hated them for that. To find out now none of that is true… I have to find the truth."

"I'll help you. Laurel will eventually come to terms. Hopefully, when all of this comes out, she'll be one step closer to healing."

Stepping away from him, Sara went to the sink and filled a saucepan with water for tea. "The things your mother said. About Nancy…" She put the pan on the flame then turned to face him. "Did you have a child with your wife?"

Chapter Thirteen

The question shouldn't have shocked him, but it did. Just hearing the words aloud was like the blade of a knife running across his chest, cutting him open, tearing out his heart. If things had turned out differently that night, he would have had a child with her.

But Nancy had died that night. And while Nick had held her in his arms, unable to help her, watching her broken body bleed out, he'd not only lost the love of his life, but his child.

"Nancy was two months pregnant when she died in that car accident." The voice that croaked out the words sounded nothing like his own.

Sara stood ten feet away, watching him. But the distance between them felt more like a mile. "Oh, Nick, I'm sorry. I didn't know."

"My mother is the only person I told about the baby. Nancy had had a miscarriage just a year before. We'd decided to wait until she was through her first trimester before making the announcement."

"That must have been awful for you."

Even after a year Nick could barely bring himself to think of that night. He'd been on call and was the first responder on the scene. Seeing her battered and bleeding body had fundamentally changed him, ripped something inside him that could never be repaired. It was a nightmare he never wanted to repeat. It was the reason he'd sworn he would never love another human being, he would never love another woman. He would never put his heart and soul on the line and risk having fate chop it to bits.

He'd always believed being alone was a far better fate than being subjected to that kind of hell. Then came Sara Douglas with her enduring love for a world that could be cruel—and a smile that could melt even the most isolated of hearts.

"Do you want to talk about it?"

He didn't. But Nick knew they would

eventually have to. He couldn't stick his head in the sand and let things continue the way they were. Maybe he'd been in denial, but there was more going on between him and Sara than he wanted to admit. He owed her the truth. When the time came for him to walk away, he wanted to be able to do it with a clear conscience.

"Come here." Picking up both their wineglasses, he carried them to the coffee table and sat on the sofa.

Sara followed and sat down beside him, not touching, but close enough so that he was keenly aware of her. He could smell her floral and musk perfume….

"You didn't realize you were dealing with damaged goods, did you?" he asked.

"I don't believe you're damaged goods."

He fell silent, remembering, trying to put the images running through his head into words. "I got the call at dark fall," he began. "A motorist had seen a car go off the coast highway. They didn't know the make of the car, so I had no idea it was Nancy. I wasn't expecting her home for another hour or so."

"My God."

"I arrived on the scene before the paramedics. The car had gone through the guardrail and plummeted about a hundred feet in a rugged area. I didn't think anyone could have survived, but you never know. I'm EMT-certified so I grabbed my kit and a thermal blanket and hiked down."

Even now, the memory of that initial shock of recognition elicited a cold sweat on the back of his neck. "The car was badly mangled, but I recognized it immediately. Nancy had been thrown from the vehicle, and I found her about twenty yards away."

Vaguely, he was aware of Sara's hand covering his. He wanted badly to take comfort in that small connection. But his mind wouldn't let him as he relived the most horrific moment of his life all over again.

"She was semi-conscious, bleeding, hurting." He swallowed the lump that had formed in his chest. "I wanted to hold her, but she was too…broken. I couldn't risk moving her without a backboard. She kept looking at me, but she couldn't speak. Her eyes…her expression…I felt so helpless because there was nothing I could do to help her."

A sigh shuddered out of him. "I got on my cell, told the paramedics to hurry. I covered her with the blanket. I talked to her. I lied to her, told her she was going to be all right. But I knew she wasn't."

Sara squeezed his hand. "In a situation like that, all you can do is give hope and comfort. Nick, I'm sure you did both of those things."

"I held her hand. It was so cold and limp in mine. It seemed to take forever for the paramedics to get there. She died before they arrived." His voice broke and he fell silent.

A big part of him hadn't wanted to share this with her; he didn't want her to know his demons. But another part of him knew it was the first step to warning her off. Already, he was feeling too much. Not only on a physical level, but emotionally as well. An emotional attachment to a woman was the one thing Nick could not allow.

Beside him, Sara turned to face him. Nick didn't look at her; he didn't want her to see the emotions he knew were emblazoned on his face. But he caught the shiny wetness of tears on her cheeks.

"You lost two people that night," she said. "I can only imagine how horribly difficult that must have been."

"You've suffered your share of loss."

She was silent for a moment, then lifted her hand as if to touch him. "Yes, I have. But everyone experiences grief differently. The one thing I do know for certain is that time really is the great healer."

He jolted when her fingertips made contact with his jaw. "I haven't…been with anyone since," he whispered. "I haven't wanted to." He finally made eye contact with her.

When he did, looking into the clear depths of her eyes was like seeing the light of sunrise after a long, dark and stormy night. It was as if he could breathe again after being oxygen-deprived.

"Until now," he whispered.

"Being with someone…Nick, it's a big step."

Turning to face her, he set both hands on either side of her face. For the span of several heartbeats, he let her beauty, both inside and outside, sink into him, warm the coldness of his soul. "That's why I needed to tell you about Nancy and the baby. I'm not…I don't have it together yet, Sara. I'm working on it, but there's a big part of me missing. A big chunk that was just ripped away that day, and I haven't been able to get it back."

"It's okay," she whispered.

"Is it okay?" he returned. "Is it okay for me to look at you and want you so badly I feel it all the way to my bones? Is it okay for me to feel that way, knowing I'm not whole? That I'm probably not capable of giving back?"

"Or maybe you don't realize how much you give back."

It was one of the kindest things anyone had ever said to him. But Nick didn't believe it. "There's nothing left inside me to give. I'm tapped out. Spent. Grief did that to me. One of us gets the short end of the stick."

"Maybe we should take it slowly." She started to rise, but he grasped her hand and pulled her back onto the sofa.

Suddenly, he couldn't bear the thought of her walking away. From this moment. From him. He knew it wasn't fair. But the need was diamond-sharp and cutting him with every beat of his heart.

He didn't want this precious moment in time to slip away. If Nick had learned anything in the last year, it was that the now is what counted.

"Is this slow enough?" he asked, and lowered his mouth to hers.

THE KISS shocked her system. Pleasure short-circuited the synapses firing in her brain. Every nerve ending in her body sizzled and snapped. All she could think was that she'd stepped out of the shallows and into the deep.

At the age of twenty-seven, she'd been kissed by plenty of men in her lifetime. She'd had two serious, albeit tepid relationships that had ended through no fault of her own. She was no stranger to passion or the pleasures of being intimate with a man.

But Nick's kiss was like nothing she'd ever experienced. On a physical level, he elevated the act to an art form that made every erogenous zone in her body weep for more. On an intellectual level, she understood fully the emotional risk he was taking.

The fact that he was willing to put his own painful past aside to get close to her shattered the last of her reservations and tore down the protective walls she'd erected around her heart.

He kissed her long and hard and so thoroughly she forgot to breathe. She didn't know if it was the lack of oxygen or the rush of blood from her head to other areas of her body that made the room dip and spin. His focus was total and so intense she couldn't catch her breath.

They were sitting on the sofa, angled so that they were face to face. A gasp escaped her when he eased her back and came down on top of her. All the while he was kissing her as she'd never been kissed before in her life. Need such as she'd never known fired inside her, flames licking higher and higher.

Vaguely, she was aware of thunder outside the bungalow. While the wind and rain lashed the windows, she and Nick dealt with their own storm inside.

He deepened the kiss, and she opened to him, inviting him inside. She could feel his labored breaths against her cheek. His muscles trembling against hers. She could feel her own ragged breaths tearing from her throat.

"I want more of you," he said darkly. "More of this."

His words whispered through her brain like a sigh. But Sara was beyond answering. Beyond rational thought. The only information her brain processed at that moment was the feel of his body against hers and the insistent pressure of his mouth.

A sigh escaped her when his hand closed over her breast. Even before she realized she was going to respond, her back arched, giving him full access. He slipped his hands beneath her shirt. With a flick of the wrist, he opened the front closure of her bra.

Her breath left her lungs in a rush when he cupped her. She nearly came up off the sofa when he trapped her nipples between his thumbs and forefingers. Sara had never considered herself a sexual person. She'd always been shy and reserved, able to go months without so much as a sexual thought. Nick had changed all of that with a single kiss and a touch so powerful it made her forget who she was.

Sara writhed beneath his ministrations. Her breasts ached. Her entire body seemed to be on fire, burning from the inside out.

Sitting back slightly, Nick looked at her. Sara stared back at him, aware of the sweat beaded on his forehead. But it was his eyes that unnerved her, that made her want with such intensity that it verged on pain.

"You're beautiful," he whispered and reached for her shirt.

A protest died on her lips when he gently pulled her shirt over her head. Her bra lay open, exposing her breasts. Feeling vulnerable, Sara moved to cover herself with her arms, but Nick stopped her. "I want to see you," he said and ducked his head.

A cry erupted in her throat when his mouth closed over her nipple. Sensation rushed the length of her body, pooling and spreading like wildfire. Vanity forgotten, she reached for him, her fingers fumbling on the buttons of his shirt.

"I want to see you, too," she whispered.

Nick obliged by ripping open his shirt. Buttons popped and fell to the floor. Sara caught a glimpse of dark hair, rounded pectoral muscles and an abdomen as hard and flat as granite. Then he was working off the shirt and pulling her to him.

His chest pressed against hers, bringing forth another rise of arousal. She could feel it pulsing between her legs, her panties going damp.

She hadn't intended for the situation to go this far. Kissing was one thing. It was safe. Controlled. But having sex with Nick Tyson was going to be something else altogether.

But Sara wasn't going to stop. For better or for worse, she wanted this precious time with him. Wanted it more than she wanted her next breath.

His arms went around her shoulders and back. Crushing her to him, he kissed her full on the mouth. Sara wrapped her arms around his shoulders, marveling at the hard-as-stone feel of his muscles. She kissed him back with an abandon she hadn't known existed inside her.

Nick pulled away and rose. Puzzled, Sara looked up at him. "Come here," he said, extending his hand to her.

The next thing she knew he swept her into

his arms. She wrapped her arm around his shoulders. With the other she cupped his cheek and turned his face toward her for a kiss. Hugging her against him, he kissed her hard, his tongue sliding into her mouth and going deep. She could feel him trembling now and it pleased her to know she had the same profound effect on him as he did on her.

He pushed open the bedroom door with his foot. The door swung wide and he stepped inside, not bothering to turn on the light. Midway to the bed, he let Sara slide from his arms. The instant her feet hit the floor, his hands were all over her, seeking, exploring.

Sara felt as if she were drowning in sensation. She'd never known what it was like to want with such ferocity. Her fingers trembled violently as she worked to open his belt. When it came away she fumbled with the zipper of his jeans. He'd removed his shirt. She couldn't keep her eyes off the dark thatch of hair and sinewy muscle. He had the most magnificent chest she'd ever laid eyes on.

He worked the bra from her shoulders.

His fingers brushed at the sensitive flesh of her belly when he unzipped her jeans. Sara's legs trembled so violently, she wasn't sure she could step out of them, but she managed.

Wearing nothing more than her panties, she moved to climb onto the bed. But Nick stopped her. Taking her hand, he turned her to face him. Light bled in through the partially open door. Sara could see the dark shadows of his eyes. The taut slant of his mouth. He was fully aroused, his breathing rushing out as if he'd just run a mile.

Dipping his head slightly, he took her mouth in a kiss. He might as well have doused her body with gasoline and tossed a match because Sara went up in flames. Her blood felt superheated, as if it were searing her veins. She kissed Nick with wild abandon. Locking her hands with his, he backed her toward the wall.

Her back made contact, but that didn't stop him. He kept coming until he pressed full length against her. Sara's senses spun with overload. There was too much sensation. Too much pleasure. Her brain couldn't seem to process it all.

But her body could.

A sigh slid from her lips when he took her hands and slid them along the wall so that they were above her head. He captured her sigh with his mouth, stealing her breath, the last of her rational thought.

Moving his right hand lower, he slid her panties downward. Sara could feel his hand trembling against her. She wanted to tell him everything was going to be all right. That she was nervous, too. But she was so caught up in the moment, her voice failed her. All she could do was speak to him with her body.

Her panties fell away. She gasped when he lifted her, wedging himself between her knees and pressing her against the wall. He took her mouth with a hunger that verged on insanity. At the same time he slid into her center and went deep.

The shock of pleasure wrenched a cry from her throat. Lurching forward, she opened, took him more deeply inside her. He began to move in long, slow strokes, and the room spun into gray.

Chapter Fourteen

Nick leaned back into the pillow and watched the light from the candle flicker and dance on the ceiling. Next to him, Sara slept with the soundness of an exhausted child. After being alone for so long, he should have taken comfort in the warmth of her body against his and the steady rhythm of her breathing. He should be enjoying the after-glow of one of the most erotic nights of his life.

But Nick was troubled. He'd been lying next to her for nearly three hours, sleepless, unable to turn off his mind. Dawn was less than an hour away now. He wanted to believe he was just keyed up from a night of intense lovemaking. But he was honest enough with himself to admit the problem was a hell of a lot more complicated than the aftereffects of mind-blowing sex.

Sara was everything a man could ever want in a life partner and more. She was funny and intelligent and sexy as hell. She could be maddeningly stubborn and head-strong, but her flaws balanced her good points and only made him want her more. He should have been overjoyed that he'd been lucky enough to find her.

But then that was the heart of the problem. After Nancy's death, Nick had sworn he would never lay his heart on the line again. That kind of love was too fragile. He knew all too well that fate could dole out unfath-omable grief and loss. Nick needed to keep his life on an even keel. Perhaps he would be willing to risk falling in love if he'd had more time to heal. But it had only been a year. Lying in the semidarkness, his heart in turmoil, the thought of love sent a cold blade of fear right through his center.

God in heaven, was it possible he'd fallen in love with Sara in the short time he'd known her?

He actually heard his breathing rate

increase as the realization bled into his psyche. His heart began to pound. Sweat slicked his forehead....

"Nick?"

Not wanting her to see him like this, Nick sat up and swung his legs over the side of the bed. He put his face in his hands and tried to get a grip. His body jolted when she set her hand on his arm.

"My God, you're trembling." Sitting up, she pulled the covers to her chest. Concern showed in her eyes when she made eye contact. "What's wrong?"

He didn't want to look at her. Didn't want her to know he was falling for her and that the thought sent him into a state of unadulterated terror.

"I'm fine," he snapped. "Leave it alone."

"Was it a dream?"

Dislodging her hand from his arm, he stood. He found his jeans draped over the chair and yanked them on. "No."

"Then what's going on?"

Nick started for the living room. He had to get out of there. Away from her questions, her misplaced concern and the kind of temptation even a cautious man couldn't resist. He didn't need her. Didn't want what she represented in his life. Damn it, he needed things to be on an even keel and she was screwing it up for him.

At the counter, Nick immersed himself in the simple chore of making coffee. He scooped beans and poured water and tried not to think of what he'd let happen.

"Nick."

He didn't want to turn and face her. He didn't want to look into her eyes and see caring and concern and an array of other emotions he couldn't reciprocate. He didn't want her to see what he knew was written all over his face. Or feel the heady pull of desire every time he laid eyes on her.

"Go back to bed," he said.

"What's wrong?"

When he didn't respond, she crossed to him, grasped his arm and turned him to her. "Talk to me. Please."

She wore the denim shirt he'd worn the night before. The hem fell to mid-thigh. The sleeves were too long and covered her hands. Beneath the denim, he saw curves he didn't want to acknowledge. Soft flesh and secret places. Worst of all, he saw compassion in her eyes and another emotion he didn't want to name.

He didn't know what to say. Didn't think he could put into words the emotions banging around inside him. He cared about her more than he wanted to. More than was wise. They'd made love twice, but already he wanted her again. He knew it was selfish and stupid and self-centered, but part of him was angry with her for doing that to him.

"What happened between us was amazing." God, he sounded like an idiot. "But I'm in no frame of mind to be getting tangled up right now."

Her eyes narrowed, her expression went wary. "I didn't realize we were tangled up."

"Let me spell it out for you then," he snapped. "I've been a widower for a year. I'm not ready to jump into any kind of relationship."

"Nick, we're friends. Last night…was spontaneous. It doesn't have to happen again if we don't want it to."

That she was being so reasonable only served to make him angrier. Couldn't she see that this had been a bad idea? Couldn't she see it would end badly? Nick wasn't ready to have his heart ripped out of his chest again. Not in this damn lifetime.

"We had sex, Sara. It was good. Damn good. But it was a mistake."

"Where is this coming from?" she asked.

"Doesn't matter. This is the way it's got to be. The way I want it. I'm sorry if I gave you the wrong impression."

"You mean as you were tearing my clothes off and whispering sweet nothings in my ear?" She choked out a sound of disbelief. "Tell me where this is coming from."

"I needed you." Nick steeled himself against the pain in her eyes, reminded himself things were better this way. "I needed...to be close. You were here."

Raising her hands as if to fend him off, she stepped away. "Don't you dare denigrate what happened between us."

"I'm being truthful."

"You're being a son of a bitch, and I don't understand why."

He latched on to the spark of anger he saw in her eyes. He *wanted* her angry. Wanted her to lash out. Wanted her to *hate* him. God knew he deserved it. It was safer for her to hate him than it was for her to love him....

"If you want to go another round I can accommodate you."

Her eyes widened when Nick started toward her. She took a step back, but he trapped her at the counter, locked her in with both arms. He ducked his head to kiss her, but she turned her head. "Cut it out," she snapped.

"Come on," he whispered, hating himself.

"Nick, I don't know what game you're playing, but this is not you."

"What you see is what you get." He tried to kiss her again. "Come on…"

"Stop it." Shoving him away, she ducked beneath his arm and fled to the guest bedroom.

Nick held his ground in the kitchen, wishing there was another way to do this. There was, of course, but he had neither the energy nor the inclination. He knew if he spent any more time with her, they would wind up in bed and he would be hopelessly lost.

No, he thought. Better to drive her away

now. Make a clean break so no one got hurt. He wasn't ready for anything more complicated. He was certainly in no frame of mind to get tangled in a relationship. She deserved better. Nick figured he could still oversee the case. He'd assign his officer to watch her and keep her safe until she left.

He found her in the guest bedroom, lugging her suitcase onto the bed. The look of hurt in her eyes just about undid him, but he didn't go to her. "I'll drive you to the bed-and-breakfast in town," he said.

She yanked open the zipper. "I'll drive myself."

"Look, I may be a jerk, but we both know it would be silly for you to go out alone this time of morning."

She glared at him over the top of the suitcase. "Like you care."

More than you'll ever know. "I want to make sure you're safe."

"You want to keep yourself safe."

The words struck a note, but he didn't let himself react. He stared at her, wondering if she had any idea how desperately he wanted to go to her.

The chirp of his cell phone interrupted. Growling, he yanked it from the clip on his belt. "Yeah."

"Chief?" B.J.'s voice came on the line. "Call just came in about a possible 10-50F on the coast highway."

The Cape Darkwood PD used the ten-code system. A 10-50F was a traffic accident with a possible fatality. "When?"

"Sometime last night." The officer paused. "I hate to be the bearer of bad news, Chief. But the caller said there's a red Mercedes convertible at the bottom of a ravine."

Red Mercedes convertible.

The description echoed in his head. His mother drove a red Mercedes convertible. She would have taken the coast road back to town last night.

The knowledge sent a rush of adrenaline through his system. "Dispatch paramedics. Call the highway patrol."

"They're en route. ETA ten minutes."

"Where did it happen?"

"Half a mile north of Fall River Road."

The words hit him like a punch to the solar plexus. It was the exact place where Nancy had lost control and gone over the edge and into a ravine.

"I'm on my way."

Nick disconnected, his heart pounding. He looked at Sara to find her eyes already on him. "I have to leave," he heard himself say.

"What happened?" she asked.

"There was an accident. On the coast highway." Mechanically, he strode to the hall closet and pulled out a slicker. "Description of the vehicle matches my mother's car. I have to go."

She came out into the hall and stood behind him. "How bad?"

"I don't know." Nick wanted to say more. He wanted to put his arms around her and take back all the cruel things he'd said and done. More than anything he didn't want to come back and find the bungalow empty.

"Don't go anywhere," he said.

She said nothing, but he could tell by the look in her eyes she would be gone by the time he got back.

"Don't leave, damn it. I'm sorry. I want to talk this out."

When he reached out to take her hand, she stepped back. "I hope your mother's all right."

Knowing there was nothing more he could do, Nick turned and headed for the door.

THE SLAM of the door echoed inside Sara's heart, bringing with it the deep ache of loneliness. Her mind whirled with news of the accident and the terrible possibility that Nick's mother had been hurt or killed. She prayed it wasn't so. He'd already endured so much loss. How much could one man take?

That brought her back to the situation at hand. The scene between her and Nick replayed in her mind, his words cutting a second time. She knew what he'd been trying to do: push her away by hurting her. She knew he was still recovering from the deaths of his wife and their unborn child. What she didn't understand was why it had to be all or nothing.

He'd hurt her tonight. He'd made love to her and then he'd treated her like dirt. Deep inside, Sara knew he hadn't meant it. But he *had* intended to hurt her. The smartest thing she could do now was give him some space.

Still, her heart ached as she gathered her things and tossed them into the suitcase. She resolved to drive until she found a motel. Then she was going to expose the truth about what had happened that night twenty years ago. She didn't need Nick to do it.

She was midway to the front door when her cell phone trilled. "Hello?"

"Sara Douglas? I'm sorry to bother you so early. This is Brett Stocker. I met you yesterday."

"Hello, Mr. Stocker." Wariness rose inside her, and she wondered why he would be calling her when he'd practically thrown them from the house the day before. "What can I do for you?"

"I'm trying to reach Chief of Police Nick Tyson. He's not answering the cell phone number he gave me."

"He's out on a call. Is there something I can help you with?"

"Well, I wanted to see if Mr. Tyson could meet with me. I found something very disturbing at my father's home. I need to get it to the authorities."

"What did you find?"

"Let me preface by saying I don't believe a damn thing you guys said yesterday about my father. He's a good and decent man. But…this… My God."

"Mr. Stocker, what did you find?"

"After you guys left, I went into my father's loft. It's an office of sorts he hasn't used for years. I was going through the desk, and I found a manuscript."

The hairs at her neck prickled. "What kind of manuscript?"

"Well, it's sort of a true-crime book. Not quite finished. I started to read, but the damn thing chilled me to the bone. Scared the hell out of me, in fact."

"Who's the author?"

"Nicholas Tyson collaborating with Richard and Alexandra Douglas."

Sara's heart was beating so hard that for a moment she couldn't speak. "My parents."

"The authors contend that my father was a monster." He choked out the words as if they were poison. "There's got to be some kind of mistake. I'd like to clear it up before this gets into the wrong hands. There's no way he did the things the authors insinuate."

"I'd like to see the manuscript."

"I'm not sure that's a good idea. It's pretty…inflammatory. I've already taken a copy to my lawyer, but I wanted the police to see it, too. I'm disputing all of it. And I'll sue to protect my father."

Sara's mind whirled with ways she might be able to gain his cooperation. "I can meet you at the police station."

He sighed. "I can't talk to the police until I've heard from my lawyer."

"Mr. Stocker, I want to see the manuscript."

He sighed. "Look, I'm about an hour from Cape Darkwood. I can meet you."

It surprised her that he would make the drive without calling first. But she imagined the contents of the manuscript had rattled him badly. To discover the man who'd raised you was a killer…

Sara glanced at her watch. Not yet seven o'clock. "It's still early. Most of the restaurants and cafés in town are only open for lunch." Her mind spun through alternate meeting places. She didn't want him at Nick's. "I can meet you at my parents' home." She rattled off directions.

"I expect strict confidentiality," he said. "I don't want to destroy my father's reputation over unfounded rumors and hearsay."

Sara thought of the eight-millimeter tape she and Nick had watched. "All I want to do is find the truth."

"I can live with that." He paused. "I can be there in about an hour."

"See you then," Sara said and disconnected.

Chapter Fifteen

Sara couldn't believe Brett Stocker had found the manuscript. What was it doing at the Stocker estate? Had the old man been hiding it all these years?

She tried to call Nick twice on the drive to the mansion. Both times she got voice mail and left detailed messages. She tried not to imagine him climbing down some ravine to find his mother's car…or maybe her body. Looking back, even though she'd been angry with him, she wished she'd gone with him. She wouldn't have been able to help with the rescue or retrieval efforts. But at least he wouldn't have had to face this alone.

The sky over the Pacific Ocean churned with purple thunderheads when she pulled into the driveway of the mansion. The morning was cool and crisp, but she knew a storm brewed over the sea and would soon make its way inland.

She let herself in through the front door and walked to the kitchen. Exhaustion tugged at her as she made coffee. She tried to figure out the best way to handle Stocker and the manuscript. First and foremost, she wanted possession of the book. She wanted its contents verified and made public. If her suspicions were correct, the book would exonerate her father once and for all.

But even with the case about to explode, Sara couldn't stop thinking about Nick. About what he could be facing at this very moment. Of all the things they'd shared the night before.

Only fifteen minutes had passed since she'd spoken to Stocker. With another forty-five minutes to kill, she carried her mug of coffee to the patio and looked out over the sea. The storm clouds roiled threateningly on the horizon, as violent and unpredictable as the sea. Even though the sun had risen in the east, the sky remained overcast.

Reaching for her cell phone, she tried Nick

one more time. Three rings and she got voice mail. "Nick, it's Sara. I hope you're okay. Call me. It's important." Sighing, she disconnected.

Sipping coffee, she wandered the mansion and found herself in her father's study. She let her mind take her back to her childhood. She and Sonia had been incorrigible children. Standing alone in a room that had once been so filled with life, Sara could practically hear the laughter. She recalled the day when Sonia dared her to climb Daddy's bookcases. Using the shelves as rungs, Sara had climbed all the way to the ceiling.

I did it, Sonia! See? Look at me! You owe me a quarter!

Twelve feet above the floor, looking out at the tops of her father's bookcases, young Sara had noticed the loose board. Looking inside, she'd found a cache of papers and jewelry and she'd felt very grown-up and important. "Wow! Look at this!"

That was when her father had come in and lovingly called her his climbing little monkey. He'd reached out and Sara had gone into his arms. He'd tickled her until she'd cried uncle.

Until this moment she'd forgotten all about the compartment above the bookcases.

Glad there was no one around to see her, Sara found the right bookcase, then grabbed onto the shelf and pulled herself up, praying it would hold her weight. She knew it was probably a waste of time. After all, Brett Stocker had the manuscript. But who knew what she'd find? More notes? A piece of her mother's jewelry?

Reaching the top of the bookcase, Sara blew dust and removed the loose panel. Her heart tripped when she spotted the thick stack of paper. *A manuscript.* Was it the same one Blaine claimed to have? Or was there a *second* book?

Next to the manuscript, an emerald pendant winked up at her. She knew immediately it had belonged to her mother; Sara had been with her father the day he'd bought it for her. Mounted in a gold setting, it was one of the most exquisite pieces of jewelry she'd ever seen. Her father had given it to her mother for Christmas. Little did they know it would be their last Christmas together.

Shoving the melancholy thoughts aside,

Sara dropped the necklace into her pocket and turned her attention back to the manuscript. The mound of paper was yellowed with age, but intact. Dust motes spewed as she lifted it.

The sheets had once been bound with a rubber band, but the band had long since snapped. The paper felt damp and heavy. Much of it was gray with mildew, the edges frayed. She almost couldn't believe she'd found it.

Quickly, she skimmed the first page. *Hollywood's Darkest Secret: A True Crime Uncovered by Nicholas Tyson and Alexandra and Richard Douglas.*

Anxious to take a peek at the manuscript, Sara climbed down the shelves, grabbed her coffee and went to the kitchen. At the counter, she set down the book and turned the first page.

In the acknowledgments, Nicholas Tyson went to great lengths to thank her parents for their expertise, insights and amateur sleuthing skills. He wrote: "By the time this book is published, Blaine Stocker will be incarcerated…."

The manuscript detailed how a talented

Hollywood director of over fourteen films became a victim of his own dark desires. How, at an age when most men were about to retire, Blaine Stocker began preying on young women hoping for a glamorous Hollywood career, only to find themselves the victim of a madman.

"Oh my God," she whispered as she flipped the pages.

The first chapter detailed the history of the first young woman to fall victim to Stocker's trap. A young woman from the wrong side of the tracks who'd been trying for years to break into acting. She'd made a fatal mistake when she'd believed Stocker's claim that he could help her. She agreed to a photo shoot in Hollywood and was never heard from again.

Tyson wrote: "Richard Douglas and I drove to Blaine's so-called studio. I've seen a lot of things in the course of my true-crime-writing career, but I've never seen anything as horrific as what was left of one of Blaine Stocker's victims."

Shaken by the words, Sara closed the manuscript and stepped back, her mind reeling. From all accounts, it seemed as if she and Nick had been right. Her parents and Nicholas Tyson had written a tell-all book that promised to ruin Blaine Stocker.

"Is that why you killed them, you son of a bitch?" Her voice sounded strange in the silence of the old house. But she knew she was right. The only questions that remained unanswered were, who had contacted her and why? Who'd left the bizarre threats? And who had stolen the notes and nearly pushed her off the cliff?

Knowing she was close to some profound revelation, Sara resolved to take everything to Nick. For the time being, they were going to have to put their personal issues aside and work together to solve this thing once and for all.

She was in the process of shoving the manuscript into her briefcase when a voice from behind spun her around.

"I see you found it."

Brett Stocker stood ten feet away. Water dripped from a dark raincoat. His hair was plastered to his head. For a split second she had the oddest sensation of déjà vu.

Outside, the storm had arrived in full force.

Rain and wind lashed at the windows like frantic fingers pleading for her to get out of there before it was too late.

Staring at the gun in Stocker's hand, she knew it was already too late.

NICK SPOTTED the skid marks a quarter mile from where Nancy's car had gone off the highway a year earlier. Turning on the cruiser's overhead strobe lights, he parked well off the highway and set up flares. On the west side of the road, the guardrail had been plowed over. A path as wide as a car cut through low-growing brush and disappeared toward the rocky shore below.

One thing Nick knew for certain. Whoever had gone over that guardrail hadn't survived.

He'd broken every speed limit on the way to the scene. The paramedics hadn't yet arrived. Intellectually, Nick knew there would be little he could do even if he was able to reach the victim. But there was no way he could stand up here and do nothing. His mother could be lying down there, broken and dying alone.

Throwing on his slicker, Nick quickly

secured a rappelling rope to the trunk of a sturdy sapling and started down the steep ravine. He fought his way through prickly brush, sliding through mud and over rain-slicked rock. A hundred feet down, he heard the hiss of steam coming from an engine. Twenty-five more feet and he reached the wreckage.

Nick let go of the rope and faced the scene. The car lay on its side, the undercarriage visible from where he stood. The smells of gasoline and burning rubber filled the air. Steam rose from beneath the twisted hood. The car was red, but it was too mangled for him to discern the make. Still, all he could think was that his mother was inside, and it was up to him to get her out.

Nick fought his way around to the other side of the vehicle. As he drew near and the front end came into view, he realized the car was not a red Mercedes, but an older Chevy. Bracing himself, he looked inside. But the driver was nowhere in sight.

"What the hell?"

For an instant, Nick stood there looking around, assuming the driver hadn't worn a safety belt and had been ejected. But there was no blood. No sign anyone had been inside. Withdrawing the flashlight from his belt, he shone it around the interior. A quiver of uneasiness went through him when he spotted the length of wood braced against the accelerator. The other end had been duct-taped to the seat.

Realization dawned in a rush of horrible clarity.

"Sara," he whispered and began to claw his way back up the ravine.

"DON'T LOOK SO surprised."

Sara stared at the pistol, her mind spinning through all the reasons Brett Stocker could be pointing it at her. But deep inside she knew.

"I don't understand," she managed.

"Aw, come on. The dots aren't that hard to connect, are they?" His gaze flicked to the manuscript on the counter. "Did you have a look-see?"

"I read enough to know your father is a cold-blooded killer."

"Yes, he is."

The answer surprised her; she hadn't expected him to agree with her. So why was he here aiming that gun at her heart? "What I can't figure is how you play into the story. You were just a kid when all of this took place."

"Like you, it took me a while to figure out what had happened. Not the kind of thing the folks talk about over Sunday-morning eggs Benedict, you know? But I eventually pieced things together." His laugh was bitter. "I knew my old man had a streak of mean, but I had no idea he was also sick."

Sara slid her hand toward her cell phone, which was clipped to her belt. If she could dial 911 without being seen… "Then why go to all this trouble to protect his secret?"

"I'm not doing it to protect him." He gave an animated laugh. "I'm doing it for the manuscript."

"But you already have the manuscript. You told me so on the phone."

He clucked, a parent gently scolding a slow child. "I lied." His gaze once again went to the manuscript on the counter. "That's the only copy. The original. The one I've been looking for."

"You're not doing this to protect your father."

"Do you have any idea how explosive the information contained in that manuscript is? Do you have any idea what that kind of information is worth? Good God, I've been trying to write a bestseller my entire adult life."

"You're doing it for the money? The fame?" Sara slowly eased the cell phone from its case. "What are you going to do? Sell it to the highest bidder?"

"Silly, silly woman." He clucked his tongue. "Think big. We're talking headlines. A *New York Times* bestseller. I can see it now." He raised his hand as if placing letters on some invisible billboard. "Son Writes Tell-All Book, Puts Hollywood-Director Father Behind Bars."

"You're going to claim authorship?" Struggling not to make her movement visible, she began to feel for the numbers with her fingertip.

"Give the lady a star." He shifted the gun to her face. "Take your hand off that damn cell phone. *Now!*"

Sara raised both hands. "Brett, don't do this."

"Toss me the phone. Do it!"

The last thing Sara wanted to do was part with her phone. It was her only connection to the outside world. Her last connection to Nick. But with a gun leveled at her head, she didn't have a choice.

Her hand shook as she unclipped the phone from her belt and tossed it to Brett. "What are you going to do with me?"

He caught the phone, turned it off and dropped it into his pocket. "I've given the subject some thought. I'm afraid this particular story isn't going to have a happy ending."

Sara knew exactly what he meant. He was going to kill her. "Don't do it, Brett. You can't possibly get away. Nick Tyson knows everything. Run while you still can."

He clucked his tongue again, looking at her as if she were a slow-witted child. "Not my style, darling. Besides, Tyson has no proof of anything." He patted the manuscript. "It's all right here and now I have it in my hands."

"You're forgetting one small detail." Sara

glanced toward the door, measured the distance between her and Stocker, wondering if she could get out before he fired a killing shot.

"What are you talking about?"

"If you kill me, you'll have a body to dispose of. A murder to explain."

"That's why you're going to commit suicide. You see, this pilgrimage into the past, the deaths of your parents, proved too much for you to bear." A smile twisted his thin mouth. "You won't be the first person to jump from these cliffs to perish on the rocks below."

"No one will believe it."

"They'll believe this." From his pocket, he produced a small folded paper and handed it to her.

Sara reached for it, her fingers closing around it. But he yanked it back at the last moment. "It's from the library printer. You were there. Now it has your prints on it." He unfolded the note and read.

To Nick and Sonia.
I'm sorry to be saying goodbye this way.
But coming back has been too much to

bear. I have too much sadness in my heart. I hope you'll forgive me. I love you both.

Sara.

He refolded the note, and for the first time she noticed the flesh-colored latex gloves he wore. "Tragic but clever, don't you think?"

"I think you're a sick bastard."

He put his hand to his chest in feigned affront. "Your harsh words wound me."

Sara could feel her heart beating out of control, the adrenaline running like wildfire through her body. Fear had taken hold of her, like a giant bird of prey gripping her with talons. She needed to think. There had to be a way out of this. But she was quickly running out of time.

Nick, where are you?

She looked at Brett Stocker, her mind whirling. "Why the phone calls?" she asked, genuinely curious. "Why did you need me here at all? You could have found the manuscript on your own and you wouldn't have had a murder to cover up."

He pointed at her as if she'd been a

naughty child. "You have no idea how difficult this has been." Not expecting her to answer, he continued. "I broke into this house several times. Being an amateur criminal, it was not easy. But I searched this old dump from top to bottom multiple times. I did this for a year, but I never found it." His eyes landed on hers and he smiled. "I knew if anyone could find it, it would be you."

But Sara's mind was already jumping ahead to other questions that had begun to spin in her head. Looking at Brett, seeing him in the raincoat with water dripping down and a gun in his hand, a flash of memory assailed her. "Your father murdered them, didn't he?"

"I always believed the theory the police had set forth. Then two years ago, after my father had his first stroke and he was lying in his hospital bed, he told me everything. He told me about the snuff films he'd made. The young women he'd murdered. He told me about the tell-all book your parents and Nicholas Tyson were working on. They were going to ruin him. Ruin everything he'd ever worked for. His reputation. They were going to send him to prison." An odd light entered Brett's eyes. "He said those women were indecent, anyway. They contributed nothing to society. No one would miss them. He said he was doing the world a favor by getting rid of them."

"That's incredibly vile," Sara said.

"But financially rewarding." Brett loosened the collar of his shirt. "My father enjoyed his just rewards, and now I'm going to enjoy mine."

Sara knew what would happen next. He would order her from the house. March her to the cliffs and force her to jump to her death.

"What about the messages?" she asked quickly.

"I have no earthly idea what you're talking about."

"Someone wrote warnings on my car. Twice. They used red finger paint."

"Obviously, it wasn't me. But then we digress. Your time is up." Raising the pistol, he pulled back the slide. "Lace your hands behind your head and walk out the door. Nice and easy. You got that?"

Sara raised her hands, but they were shaking so badly she couldn't lace them. "Brett, it doesn't have to be this way. Please. Take the manuscript and run."

"I swear I'll blow a hole in you." He jammed the gun at her. "Now walk out that door or I'll shoot you where you stand."

Chapter Sixteen

Nick retrieved his cell phone messages on the way to the bungalow. Worry notched into cold hard fear when he listened to Sara's message. He couldn't believe she was going to meet Blaine Stocker alone. He had a bad feeling about the man. Cursing, he tried her number, hoping to stop her, but the call went instantly to voice mail.

His cruiser's tires slid on wet pavement when he whipped the car into a U-turn and headed for the coast highway. He mashed the accelerator, the speedometer jumping to ninety miles per hour as he snatched up the mike and called dispatch.

Relief rippled through him when he heard B.J. on the other end. "I need backup and an ambulance at the Douglas mansion."

"Roger that, Chief." A heavy pause. "What happened?"

"Someone is trying to kill Sara. I think they're at the mansion now. No time to get into the details, but it has something to do with the murders twenty years ago." He paused to negotiate a curve, backed off the speedometer when the car fishtailed. "Get someone out there now. No lights. No siren."

"Got it."

Nick disconnected.

The so-called accident had been a ruse. He'd fallen for it hook, line and sinker. And now Sara was going to pay the price.

He wasn't going to lose her. Damn it, he wasn't going to allow it.

Rapping his fist against the steering wheel, Nick cursed himself for leaving her alone. How could he have been so stupid? How could he put his own selfish needs above her safety?

But Nick knew the answer. Nancy's death and the death of their unborn child had warped something inside him. The grief had been so achingly profound that some small protective mechanism kicked in whenever he began to feel too much for someone. He'd been willing to live a loveless and solitary existence as long as he never had to feel that gut-wrenching pain ever again.

Only now did Nick realize it had all been for nothing. At some point in the last days, he'd fallen in love with Sara. He'd done the one thing he'd sworn he would not. His heart had betrayed him. Once again, he faced the same horrific loss and grief as he had before.

"I'm not going to let this happen," he vowed between clenched teeth.

He put the pedal to the floor.

And began to pray that he wasn't already too late.

SARA COULDN'T BELIEVE her life was going to end this way. At the hands of a man whose father had murdered her parents and Nicholas Tyson in cold blood. She thought about the bogus suicide note. There was no way Sonia or Nick would believe it, particularly with the information she and Nick had just uncovered.

Nick.

The thought of him brought tears to her eyes. The image of his face filled her mind. The intimacies they'd shared just a few short hours ago. She'd fallen in love with him. The realization should have shocked her. But it didn't. Maybe in some small corner of her mind she'd always loved him. Maybe in her heart she'd always known she would come back to this place. And fate would take care of the rest. How ironic that she would realize her one and only love just moments before her death.

Rain slashed at her like cold knives as she trudged down the path toward the cliffs. She heard Brett behind her, his footfalls heavy on the ground, raindrops pattering against his raincoat. She kept hoping Nick would appear on the trail in front of them, pistol drawn, and end the nightmare. But Nick was at the scene of what was probably a horrific crash that could possibly involve his mother. There was no way he could leave. There was no way he could even know she was in trouble.

Sara was on her own. If she was going to get out of this alive, she was going to have to come up with some kind of plan. If she refused to jump, she knew Stocker would shoot her. Either way, she was going to die.

Ahead, the path curved. Beyond, the cliffs looked out over a raging sea and rocky shore a hundred feet below. If she was going to do something, now was the time. Once they reached the cliffs, it would be too late.

Sara let her foot catch on a protruding rock, feigned a stumble, and dropped to her knees. "Damn it." Grimacing as if in pain, she looked over her shoulder at Brett. "My ankle. Wait."

He raised the gun. "You've got to be kidding."

"I think I sprained it."

"I don't give a damn about your ankle. Get up. We're running out of time."

There was no way Sara was going to jump off that cliff and let him get away with murder. She knew she risked getting shot in the back if she ran, but the odds seemed better. It was a risk she was willing to take.

She struggled to rise, leaving her weight off her right foot. A few feet away, the mangled branch of a dead juniper drew her attention. It was the size of a small bat. If she could reach it, she could use it as a weapon.

"I don't think I can walk," she said.

Lowering the gun marginally, Brett grabbed her arm and yanked her forward. "Walk, bitch!"

Sara leaned heavily against him. Snarling, he shoved her away. Pretending to reach out to break her fall, she snatched up the branch and swung it as hard as she could. Stocker's eyes went wide. The gun came up, swung toward her. She caught a glimpse of his face an instant before the wood slammed against his left temple.

Screaming in pain and anger, he reeled backward, landing hard on his backside. His free hand clutched at his left eye. With his right, he brought up the gun. "You bitch!"

"No!" Sara spun to run as he leveled the weapon on her.

"Stop!" he shouted.

Sara took off like a sprinter out of a starting block. Three strides and a gunshot rent the air. A scream tore from her throat when white-hot pain shot down her arm from elbow to wrist.

Shock rippled through her when she saw blood dripping from her fingertips. It registered that she'd been shot, but she couldn't let the fear paralyze her; she couldn't let it slow her down. If she wanted to live, she was going to have to outrun him.

Her feet pounded through mud, carrying her down the trail at a dangerous speed. Branches and rain pelted her. Heat radiated down from her elbow, but her fingers had gone numb. Vaguely, she was aware of the growing bloodstain on her sleeve. Red rainwater dripping from her fingertips.

The trail forked. Realizing she needed a way to let Nick know where to find her, particularly if she lost consciousness, she reached for her mother's necklace in her pocket, plucked it out and dropped it in the center of the trail that ran parallel with the cliffs.

A second shot rang out. Instinctively, Sara ducked, glanced behind her. Ten yards back, Stocker staggered toward her, waving the gun madly. "You're *dead!*"

A scream jammed her throat when he raised the gun for another shot. Heart pounding out of control, she took the north trail.

Another shot exploded. The dull *thunk!* of a bullet striking the ground sounded at her feet. *Oh, dear God, he's going to cut me down!* she thought wildly.

The thought had barely formed in her mind when the trail ended abruptly. Beyond, the ground dropped away a hundred feet to the rocky shore below. Twenty years ago the trail had gone on for another mile or so. But erosion had eaten it away. Now, she was trapped.

Panic gripped her so hard that for a moment she was paralyzed. Glancing once over her shoulder, she caught a glimpse of Stocker through the trees, guessed him to be ten yards behind her. And she knew if she stayed put he would shoot her down.

Willing to take her chances on the rocks, Sara looked over the edge, searching desperately for a safe place to land.

Closing her eyes, she hurled herself into space.

THE FIRST GUNSHOT stopped Nick dead in his tracks. The second sent his heart into overdrive. For a moment, he stood on the trail with rain pouring all around and listened, trying to establish the direction from which the shot had come. A third shot rang out, and he knew the shooter was near the cliffs.

Not considering his own safety, he ran headlong down the trail. Rain lashed at his face. Branches tore at his clothes. But he didn't slow down. All he could think was that he was not going to lose Sara the same way he'd lost Nancy.

Twenty yards from the cliffs, the trail forked. Nick stood at the junction for the span of several heartbeats, listening, trying to decide which way to go. He'd stepped left when he spotted the spark of green against the muddy earth. Bending, he scooped up the necklace. He could tell by the lack of dirt that it had been recently dropped, and he knew immediately Sara was telling him to take the northernmost trail.

Dropping the necklace into his pocket, Nick tore down the trail. He could make out footprints, but they were quickly being washed away by the rain. He rounded a curve and the cliffs came into view. A tall man in a black raincoat stood on the ledge with his back to Nick, looking down. He held a gun in his right hand and was firing shots at something below.

What the hell?

Recognition sparked. Brett Stocker. But what the hell was Stocker doing out here? Protecting his old man? Or was this about something else?

Drawing his weapon, Nick chambered a bullet and started toward Stocker. He was midway there when the other man fired a series of shots. Realization struck Nick like a boxer's punch. Fear twisted his insides into knots. Sara had gone off the cliff. God only knew how badly she was hurt. And the son of a bitch was trying to pick her off.

Chapter Seventeen

The bullet hit the ground two inches from the ledge where Sara crouched. A foot away, the cliff dropped away to the rocky beach below.

A groan escaped her as she struggled to her feet. Pain echoed through every inch of her body. She'd landed on a ledge about two feet wide that was covered with rock and moss and the twisted roots of long-dead junipers.

Every nerve in her body jumped when another shot rang out. Sara looked up. Terror spread through her like wildfire when she saw Brett Stocker leaning over the rocky ledge above, aiming the pistol at her.

"You can't get away!" he screamed.

Another shot thwacked against the ground next to her foot. Sara looked around wildly.

But the ledge offered no cover, no place to hide. All she could do was get as close to the base of the cliff as possible and hope he wasn't a very good shot.

She staggered to the rock wall, pressed her back against it and tried to make herself as small as possible. Overhead, she could see the gun's muzzle as he tried to get it into position to kill her. In the back of her mind, Sara wondered how many bullets he had left. If he had a spare magazine.

"Help me!" she screamed. *"Help!"*

But she knew there was no one around for miles.

A cry escaped her when another bullet slammed into the ground inches from her foot. Sara danced sideways, pressed her body harder into the rock behind her, wishing desperately she could melt into it. It was a hopeless situation. She was a sitting duck. Stocker had a bad angle to contend with. But it was only a matter of time before one of his bullets found its mark.

Nick, where are you? she thought.

The only answer she got was the crash of the surf below and the retort of another gunshot.

NICK'S VISION tunneled on Stocker. The roar of rain and the surf faded to silence. He didn't let himself think about what he was going to do. He didn't consider consequences. His own safety never entered his mind. Nothing mattered except for saving the woman he loved.

The world went silent and still. Nick raised the gun, aimed for a body shot. Held it steady. "Toss the gun or I'll split you in half."

Stocker turned. His eyes went wide. Blood covered the right side of his face.

"Drop it," Nick ordered.

Stocker lifted the gun by its butt and let it fall to the ground.

"Put your hands up and turn around."

To his surprise, Stocker obeyed. Holding his sidearm steady, Nick approached. "Where is she?"

Stocker's expression twisted into that of a crazed maniac. He glanced over the cliff, a chilling smile overtaking his face.

"Sara!" Keeping an eye on Stocker, Nick approached the cliff. "Sara!"

Stocker hit him with the violence of a linebacker sacking a quarterback. An animalistic cry tore from Stocker's mouth as both men went down.

As he rolled, Nick caught a glimpse of a narrow ledge below. A flash of the rocky shore a hundred feet down. The gray, churning ocean beyond. He brought up his weapon, fired off a wild shot, missed.

Breathless with adrenaline, Nick scrambled to his feet.

Stocker rolled. An inhuman scream tore from his throat as the gun came up. Nick's finger jerked on the trigger. Once. Twice. He didn't count the number of shots. Seconds later, Stocker lay dead on the ground.

Turning away, Nick looked around. "Sara! *Sara!* Answer me, damn it!"

A thousand emotions descended when he heard her voice call out his name. He found her ten feet below, crouched against the wall of the cliff. She'd taken a serious fall, but she was standing.

His legs shook as he climbed down to her. He reached for her and she went into his arms. "Sara. My God. Are you all right?"

"Now I am," she said, resting her head against his shoulder.

Then he was shoving her to arm's-length, his eyes sweeping over her in a quick physical inventory. His heart stopped dead in his chest when he spotted blood dripping from her fingertips. "Oh, honey, you're bleeding."

"I'm hit," she said. "I don't think it's too bad."

For a moment, Nick was overcome with emotion. Unable to speak, unable to function, all he could do was wrap his arms around her and hold her against him.

She trembled violently, but he could feel her life force pulsing strong and warm. "I'm glad you're okay," he said.

"How did you find me?"

"The necklace," he said. "That was incredibly smart."

Reaching up, she cupped his face with her uninjured hand. "You saved my life."

Nick closed his eyes against a hard rush of emotion. He knew he was holding her more tightly than he should, considering her injuries. But he couldn't help it. She was alive. At the moment he didn't think he was ever going to let her go again.

Pulling away slightly, she made eye contact. "Stocker?"

He shook his head. "Dead."

"He tried to kill me," she said. "He was going to make it look like suicide. All because he wanted to claim the manuscript as his own."

"He's never going to hurt anyone ever again." He ran his fingertips down her arm, his gut tightening at the sight of the blood. "Hang tight. There's an ambulance on the way."

She offered a smile. "I'll let you know if I need to faint."

He smiled back. "You're incredibly brave."

"So were our parents."

He nodded, wiping at the tears that had begun to stream down her cheeks. "We're going to be all right," he said.

"As long as we're together," she said, "We're going to be just fine."

For the first time in what seemed like an eternity, Nick Tyson truly believed it.

Epilogue

The curtains billowed and snapped at the balcony, ushering in the scent of the sea and a warm kiss of California sunshine. Outside, gulls cartwheeled and swooped, their cries carrying like the sound of children's laughter. Beyond, the Pacific Ocean churned blue and green, capped with white in a kaleidoscope of color so lovely it took Sara's breath away.

Three weeks had passed since that terrible day on the cliffs. Brett Stocker had died at the scene from a bullet wound. The following day, his father, Blaine, had been arrested in connection with the film Sara had found. He admitted to murdering four young women twenty-five years ago and capturing their deaths on film. He also confessed to the murders of Nicholas Tyson and Alexandra and Richard Douglas, who'd been working on a tell-all book.

Sara was still recovering from the bullet wound that had grazed her left bicep. Eight stitches and she'd been released from the hospital the next day. That same morning, she'd contacted the *Cape Darkwood Press* and spent an afternoon with a young reporter hungry to make his mark in the world of journalism. The next day a front-page article shocked the community with a truth no one could ever have imagined, exonerating her father and the reputations of Nicholas Tyson and Alexandra Douglas.

Much to Sara's surprise, the young journalist had also interviewed the caretaker, and discovered Skeeter had been the one to write the warnings on her car. Not to frighten her, of course, but to warn her of the dangers. Unable to speak and frightened of the police, it was the only way he could think of to try to keep her safe. The unsettling nature of the messages was due only to his near illiteracy.

Sara had also learned what happened the day someone pushed her off the cliff. Skeeter had seen Brett Stocker snooping around the mansion. Skeeter tried to warn Sara by leaving the message on her car. He'd expected her to flee, but she'd surprised him by giving chase. Frightened, Skeeter had run toward his cottage down the beach. The caretaker later told the police that Brett Stocker had been the one to push her from the cliff.

And then there was Nick.

Just thinking of him made Sara's breath hitch. He hadn't left her side the entire time she'd been in the hospital. It had been there, in the chaos of the emergency room that he'd proposed. And it was there that Sara had accepted.

Stepping back from the mirror, she frowned. "It's too tight," she said.

"It's perfect." Sonia smoothed the waterfall of ivory satin with her palm and stepped back to admire the dress.

"The veil is crooked."

"The veil is exactly right."

"What about the bouquet?"

"Stop being so persnickety. I've got it right here."

"It's my wedding day. I've got a right to be persnickety."

Laughing, Sonia handed her sister the bouquet of salmon-colored roses. "If I didn't know better, I'd think you were nervous."

"I'm not nervous." Taking the flowers, Sara grinned. "I'm terrified."

Sonia stopped fussing with the flowers and looked at her younger sister. "Terrified of what, honey?"

"Everything. Nothing." Realizing she wasn't making any sense whatsoever, Sara choked out a laugh. "I want to get this right."

"You got the most important thing right." Sonia squeezed her shoulder. "I talked to him this morning, sis. He's so in love with you he couldn't take his eyes off the staircase where you'll be making your appearance."

The thought of Nick waiting for her downstairs calmed her frazzled nerves. "I'm crazy about him."

Stepping back, Sonia eyed the dress her younger sister wore and smiled. "You're beautiful. Mom would have loved it that you're wearing her dress."

"It feels right."

They were standing in the same room they had shared as sisters. Sara in her wedding gown, Sonia in her matron-of-honor gown. With the sun shining through the balcony doors and the ocean breeze filling the room with the scent of the sea, Sara thought it couldn't be any more perfect.

"I think Mom and Dad would have liked the wedding taking place here at the house," she said.

Sonia's eyes went misty. "Good memories to replace the bad."

"I wish they could be here."

Smiling, Sonia hugged her sister. "They are, honey."

A quiet tap on the door spun both women around. Before Sonia could answer, the door opened. Tension crept up the back of Sara's neck when Laurel Tyson appeared. She wore a soft-blue dress with matching shoes. Her tastefully coifed silver hair was piled on top of her head. She looked elegant and regal, but her eyes were melancholy.

"I hope I'm not interrupting," she said.

Sonia glanced at her sister as if to gauge her reaction.

"Come in," Sara said.

The older woman entered the bedroom.

Her eyes skimmed over Sara and her mouth curved into a rare smile. "My goodness, you're stunning."

Uncertain what to expect, Sara remained silent. Sonia went to her side, took her hand. "It was Mom's dress."

"I remember it well," Laurel said. "I was her bridesmaid of honor." She laughed. "My dress wasn't nearly as lovely."

Laurel seemed to gather her composure, then spoke. "I owe both of you an apology. If your parents were here, I'd owe them an apology as well."

Sara had suspected Laurel would come around. She just hadn't expected it so soon. She saw the same surprise on her sister's face. "Thank you," she said.

"Your mother was my best friend," Laurel said. "I loved her like a sister. It hurt to believe she betrayed me. Hurt even more to lose her." She toyed with her beaded bag. "I let that hurt turn me into a bitter old woman. Thanks to you, Sara, I don't have to be that way any more." She extended her hand. "Thank you for exposing the truth. I hope you'll accept my apology for being so awful to you. I hope even more that we can become friends."

Unable to speak for the emotions crowding into her throat, Sara reached out. Laurel took her hand and squeezed. Tears filled the woman's eyes, but she turned away and quickly left the room without speaking.

"Don't cry or you'll ruin your makeup."

Sara choked out a laugh and turned to her sister. "Thank you for being here."

"I wouldn't miss my little sister getting married for the world." Sonia hugged her tightly. A second knock at the door made her roll her eyes. "What now?"

The door swung open. Sara's heart did a little jig in her chest when she saw Nick standing in the hall. He looked strikingly handsome in his black tux.

"Don't you know it's bad luck for the groom to see the bride before the wedding?" Sonia said.

"I couldn't wait," he said. But every ounce of his focus was on Sara. She took his breath away, and for a moment he couldn't find his voice.

"You're stunning," he heard himself say.

As if realizing they needed a moment together, Sonia started for the door. "You've got five minutes, guys. I'll be in the hall."

Nick didn't hear her leave. Didn't hear the door close. Before he even realized he was going to move, he was across the room and reaching for his wife-to-be. "I couldn't wait to see you."

Sara went into his arms. Wrapping his arms around her was like coming home after a long and grueling trip. For the span of several heartbeats all Nick could do was hold her, take in her scent and thank God he'd found her again after all these years.

"If I didn't know better, I might think you missed me," Sara whispered.

"Desperately."

"Me, too."

"Was my mom nice?"

"She's kind and sweet and sad," Sara said. "We're going to be just fine." Smiling, she brushed her lips across his. "Did I thank you for saving my life the other day on the cliffs?"

"A couple of times." But Nick knew that while he might have saved her life in a physical sense, it was Sara who'd saved his in all the ways it counted. For months he'd been so blinded by grief that he hadn't been able to open his heart. Sara had changed all of it.

Pulling back slightly, he looked into her eyes, felt the floor tilt beneath his feet. "I just came up to tell you I love you."

"I'm glad you did."

"I loved you even when I was twelve and you were seven. That kiss sort of sealed the deal."

A laugh bubbled up from her throat. "Who would have thought?"

Nick gazed into her eyes, loving her so much he could barely contain the joy burgeoning in his chest. He wasn't sure why he'd been compelled to see her when they were to be married in just a few minutes. He knew they had their entire lives ahead of them. But that was the way things had become between them, and he wouldn't change it for the world.

Downstairs the first notes of the bridal march began to play. "What do you say we go get married?"

"Best idea I've heard all day," Sara said and walked with her husband-to-be toward the door.

* * * * *

Melita had been expecting a chaste quick kiss of the generic variety. But this kiss with Sully was the kind that sparked a dying flame to life. The kind of kiss you can't plan for. The kind of kiss memories are built on.

The memory of her murdered lover, Nemo, came to her then and she made a starved little noise in the back of her throat. She raised her arms and threaded her fingers through Sully's hair, pulled him closer. Felt his body settle, then melt into her.

In that instant her hunger for him grew, and his for her. She pressed herself to him with more urgency, and he responded in kind.

Melita came out of her kiss-induced memory of Nemo with a start. "Wait a minute." She pushed Sully away from her. "You bastard!"

She spit two nasty words at him in Greek, then wiped his kiss from her lips.

"I thought you deserved some solid proof that I'm still in one piece." He started for the door. "The clock's ticking, honey. Come on, let's get out of here."

"That's it? You sucker me into kissing you, and that's all you have to say?"

"I'm sorry. How's that?"

He didn't sound sorry in the least. "You're—"

"Getting out of this godforsaken prison cell. Stop whining and let's go."

"Not if I was being shot at sunrise. Go. You deserve whatever you get if you walk out that door."

He turned back. "Freedom is what I'm going to get."

"A second of freedom before the guards in the hall shoot you." She jammed her hands on her hips. "And to think I was worried about you."

"If you're staying behind, it's no skin off my ass."

"Wait! What about our deal?"

"You just said you're not coming. Make up your mind."

"Have you forgotten we need a boat?"

"How could I? You keep harping on it."

"I'm not going without a boat. And those guards out there aren't going to just let you walk out of here. You need me and we need a plan."

"I already have a plan. I'm getting out of here. That's the plan."

"I should have realized that you never intended to take me with you from the very beginning. You're a liar and a coward."

Of everything she had read, there was nothing in Sully Paxton's file that hinted he was a coward, but it was the one word that seemed to register in that one-track mind of his. The look he nailed her with a second later was pure venom.

He came at her so quickly she didn't have time to get out of his way. "You know I'm not a coward."

"Prove it. Give me until dawn. I need one more night to put everything in place before we leave the island."

"You're asking me to stay in this cell one more night...and trust you?"

"Yes."

He snorted. "Yesterday you knew they were planning to harm me, but instead of doing something about it you went to bed and never gave me a second thought. Suppose tonight you do the same. By tomorrow I might damn well be in my grave."

"Okay, I screwed up. I won't do it again." Melita sucked in a ragged breath. "I can't leave this minute. Dawn, Sully. Wait until dawn." When he looked as if he was about to say no, she pleaded, "Please wait for me."

"You're asking a lot. The door's open now. I would be a fool to hang around here and trust that you'll be back."

"What you can trust is that I want off this island as badly as you do, and you're my only hope."

"I must be crazy."

"Is that a yes?"

"Dammit!" He turned his back on her. Swore twice more.

"You won't be sorry."

He turned around. "I already am. How about we seal this new deal?"

He was staring at her lips. Suddenly Melita knew what he expected. "We already sealed it."

"One more. You enjoyed it. Admit it."

"I enjoyed it because I was kissing someone else."

He laughed. "That's a good one."

"It's true. It might have been your lips, but it wasn't you I was kissing."

"If that's your excuse for wanting to kiss me, then—"

"I was kissing Nemo."

"What's a nemo?"

Melita gave Sully a look that clearly told him that he was trespassing on sacred ground. She was about to enforce it with a warning when a voice in the hall jerked them both to attention.

She bolted away from the wall. "Get back in bed. Hurry. I'll be here before dawn."

She didn't reach the door before he snagged her arm, pulled her up against him and planted a kiss on her lips that took her completely by surprise.

When he released her, he said, "If you're confused about who just kissed you, the name's Sully. I'll be here waiting at dawn. Don't be late."

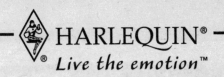

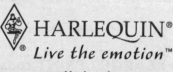

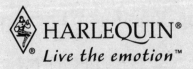

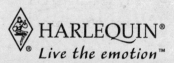

HARLEQUIN® *Presents*

The world's bestselling romance series...
The series that brings you your favorite authors,
month after month:

Helen Bianchin...Emma Darcy
Lynne Graham...Penny Jordan
Miranda Lee...Sandra Marton
Anne Mather...Carole Mortimer
Susan Napier...Michelle Reid

and many more uniquely talented authors!

Wealthy, powerful, gorgeous men...
Women who have feelings just like your own...
The stories you love, set in exotic, glamorous locations...

HARLEQUIN® *Presents*

Seduction and Passion Guaranteed!

Harlequin® Historical
Historical Romantic Adventure!

Imagine a time of chivalrous knights and unconventional ladies, roguish rakes and impetuous heiresses, rugged cowboys and spirited frontierswomen— these rich and vivid tales will capture your imagination!

Harlequin Historical... they're too good to miss!

HHDIR06